HARLEQUIN®

AMERICA *Romance*®

D0052096

MAITLAND MATERNITY

Tina Leonard

QUADRUPLETS ON THE DOORSTEP

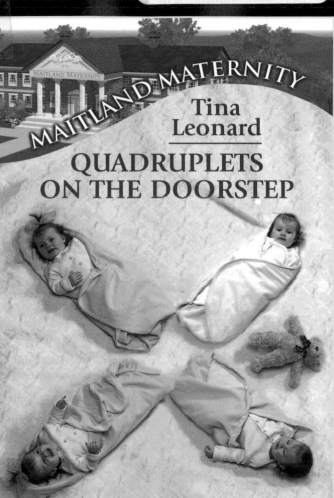

HARLEQUIN®
*M*akes any time special ®

ISBN 0-373-16905-1

9 780373 169054

50450

AVAILABLE THIS MONTH:

#905 QUADRUPLETS ON THE DOORSTEP
Tina Leonard

#906 PREACHER'S IN-NAME-ONLY WIFE
Mindy Neff

#907 PREGNANT AND INCOGNITO
Pamela Browning

#908 HIGH-SOCIETY BACHELOR
Krista Thoren

Dear Reader,

Happy New Year! Harlequin American Romance is starting the year off with an irresistible lineup of four great books, beginning with the latest installment in the MAITLAND MATERNITY: TRIPLETS, QUADS & QUINTS series. In *Quadruplets on the Doorstep* by Tina Leonard, a handsome bachelor proposes a marriage of convenience to a lovely nurse for the sake of four abandoned babies.

In Mindy Neff's *Preacher's In-Name-Only Wife*, another wonderful book in her BACHELORS OF SHOTGUN RIDGE series, a woman must marry to secure her inheritance, but she hadn't counted on being an instant wife *and* mother when her new husband unexpectedly receives custody of an orphaned baby. Next, a brooding loner captivates a pregnant single mom in *Pregnant and Incognito* by Pamela Browning. These opposites have nothing in common—except an intense attraction that neither is strong enough to deny. Finally, Krista Thoren makes her Harlequin American Romance debut with *High-Society Bachelor,* in which a successful businessman and a pretty party planner decide to outsmart their small town's matchmakers by pretending to date.

Enjoy them all—and don't forget to come back again next month when a special three-in-one volume, *The McCallum Quintuplets,* featuring *New York Times* bestselling author Kasey Michaels, Mindy Neff and Mary Anne Wilson is waiting for you.

Wishing you happy reading,

Melissa Jeglinski
Associate Senior Editor
Harlequin American Romance

Tina Leonard

QUADRUPLETS ON THE DOORSTEP

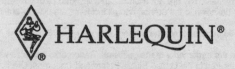

TORONTO • NEW YORK • LONDON
AMSTERDAM • PARIS • SYDNEY • HAMBURG
STOCKHOLM • ATHENS • TOKYO • MILAN • MADRID
PRAGUE • WARSAW • BUDAPEST • AUCKLAND

Special thanks and acknowledgment are given
to Tina Leonard for her contribution to the
MAITLAND MATERNITY:
TRIPLETS, QUADS & QUINTS series.

To Kasey Michaels, for being an inspiration and a friend
and to my Mimi, because she's cool.
Lisa and Dean, you guys make me smile.
Tim, I guess we've done okay so far—thanks for
doing my classwork in the first grade.
See what it got you!

RECYCLED PAPER

ISBN 0-373-16905-1

QUADRUPLETS ON THE DOORSTEP

ABOUT THE AUTHOR

Tina Leonard loves to laugh, which is one of the many reasons she loves writing Harlequin American Romance books. In another lifetime, Tina thought she would be single and an East Coast fashion buyer forever. The unexpected happened when Tina met Tim again after many years—she hadn't seen him since they'd attended school together from first through eighth grade. They married, and now Tina keeps a close eye on her school-age children's friends! Lisa and Dean keep their mother busy with soccer, gymnastics and horseback riding. They are proud of their mom's "kissy books" and eagerly help her any way they can. Tina hopes that readers will enjoy the love of family she writes about in her books. Recently a reviewer wrote, "Leonard had a wonderful sense of the ridiculous," which Tina loved so much she wants it for her epitaph. Right now, however, she's focusing on her wonderful life and writing a lot more romance!

Books by Tina Leonard

HARLEQUIN AMERICAN ROMANCE

748—COWBOY COOTCHIE-COO
758—DADDY'S LITTLE DARLINGS
771—THE MOST ELIGIBLE...DADDY
796—A MATCH MADE IN TEXAS
811—COWBOY BE MINE
829—SURPRISE! SURPRISE!
846—SPECIAL ORDER GROOM
873—HIS ARRANGED MARRIAGE
905—QUADRUPLETS ON THE DOORSTEP

HARLEQUIN INTRIGUE

576—A MAN OF HONOR

CAST OF CHARACTERS

Caleb McCallum—When the ex-cop comes across a lovely woman and four babies he decides need rescuing, he goes from brooding loner to devoted family man.

April Sullivan—The warmhearted neonatal nurse's desire to keep the abandoned quadruplets prompts her to enter a temporary marriage with the sexy bachelor.

Jenny Barrows—The teenage mother of the quadruplets wants to find a good home for her babies and knows April will give them the loving care they need.

Jackson McCallum—The founder of the McCallum Multiple Birth Wing has a special place in his heart for the quadruplets born there.

Adam and Maggie McCallum—Caleb's brother and sister-in-law hope to be parents themselves in the near future. Read about their story in *The McCallum Quintuplets*, a 3-in-1 collection coming next month.

Chapter One

Caleb McCallum peered through the glass window of the McCallum Multiple-Birth Wing Neonatal Intensive Care Unit. Four plastic isolettes were marked Baby Barrow number one, Baby Barrow number two, three and four—the four abandoned children whose case he'd been sent to monitor. A nurse moved from isolette to isolette, touching each baby gently, tucking a blanket here, replacing a baby cap there. He was caught by her loving touch as she lingered over each small form.

Caleb's mind automatically went over a previous conversation with his father. Jackson McCallum, founder of the Emily McCallum Multiple-Birth at Maitland Maternity Hospital in Austin, had commanded him to "look" in on the situation and "find out what you can. Use some of your police contacts in Missing Persons, Caleb."

"Dad, the police will handle the problem fine." He was an ex–police officer. Ex. Using his old contacts was something he'd prefer not to do, and he'd definitely not wanted any part of this latest request.

"It's my wing, son," Jackson had replied. "I feel responsible. I want to know that this young mother is found, and quickly. There are four young lives missing the most important part of their world's new beginning."

Caleb hadn't reminded his father that he knew damn well what it meant to be raised without a mother. Jackson knew it, and was trying to pull Caleb into the situation, fully aware that Caleb wouldn't want to relive any part of his former life as a cop.

"Not to mention that a young girl who's just been through a difficult birth shouldn't be out of bed, much less running around town. She needs to be in the hospital where she can be cared for. I'm worried like hell about that."

It wasn't so much that Jackson was worried about the wing's reputation. His father would be reliving the moment his beloved wife had died in childbirth—the result of giving birth to Caleb.

"All right, Dad," he'd finally said. "I'll go to the wing and do some asking around."

"Only right that you do," Jackson said. "To him whom much is given, much is demanded. It's your duty. You were the finest officer on the force."

"Were, Dad. Were." And he'd hung up the phone, but the conversation lingered, refusing to be switched off replay.

Dad did a good thing by building this wing, Caleb admitted reluctantly. Even if it did exist as a monument to the mother he'd lost, Caleb knew he should be proud of his father's generosity. But to him it signified loss, not gain.

The nurse hovering over the isolettes no doubt would disagree. He didn't think the missing real mother could spend more time nurturing those babies.

She glanced up, catching him staring at her. *She's cute,* he realized at once—*real cute.* Big green eyes assessed him in a face surrounded by long, curly auburn hair. Creamy skin dotted with light freckles across a tiny nose was accented by full, rosy lips.

Before he realized what she was doing, she'd left the nursery and come to stand beside him. She'd just reach his midchest, if she took a deep breath and stood poker-straight.

"Aren't they sweet?" she asked him.

Caleb stared at her, lost for just a moment, his gaze locked on her beautiful smile.

"They smell like...like new spring," she said dreamily. "Sometimes soapy-clean, and sometimes formula-burpy, but precious beyond words. I think of spring when I hold them, even when they smell like formula."

"It's only late December."

She gazed through the window. "You'd have to hold them to understand, I guess."

He cleared his throat, uncomfortable with the

emotions the petite nurse was setting off inside him. "Has anyone heard from the mother?"

Slowly, she turned to face him. "I'm afraid not."

Her eyes were so sad he wanted to comfort her—and yet, he was here in a more or less official capacity. The cop in him went into command. "I'm Caleb McCallum," he said, putting out a hand for her to shake.

"The son of Jackson McCallum who dedicated this wing?" she asked, sliding her hand into his. "Bri's brother?"

He nodded, registering with all his old sensory training that her skin was soft, her touch gentle, her fingers small-boned, like the fragile bones in a mourning dove's wing.

"I'm April Sullivan. It's nice to meet you."

Her hand withdrew from his, and he shoved his own into his jeans pocket. "How well did you know the mother?"

"Jenny Barrows?" Auburn eyebrows lifted quizzically. "She was here for about two weeks before she gave birth. I suppose that she preferred me to the other nurses. But I certainly didn't know her well enough for her to leave her children to me, not that I would have suspected that she was even considering such a thing."

"How did she let you know she wanted you to have them?"

"I'd laid my sweater on my chair when I went to prep a patient. Jenny left a note in my sweater pocket asking me to take care of her children. I was...shocked. I still can't believe it.''

"How many hours after the birth did you find the note and realize Ms. Barrows was missing?"

She stared at him, her eyebrows drawing into delicate crescents. "The questions you're asking are so official. You sound like the officers who've been interviewing me."

"I used to be on the police force."

"I see. And now?"

"I work as a security consultant and troubleshooter at McCallum Enterprises. Dad asked me to see how the situation is progressing."

"That's nice of you. And him."

"Why?"

"Well, to be so concerned."

"He has a strong affinity for this wing, and if he thinks there's anything he can do to help the mother once she's found, believe me, Dad will do it."

"That's kind."

If living in the past was something to be proud of, maybe. But Caleb didn't say that to April.

"I have to get back to the babies. If you'll excuse me—"

He really didn't want her to go just yet. "You didn't answer my question."

It seemed to him that she set her jaw with a tiny bit of defiance. "I found the note in my pocket at eight a.m., which would have made it four days past the delivery on Friday. She left four days before

Christmas, the babies' first Christmas,'' she said
softly. It seemed she straightened suddenly to stare
at him. ''Anything else you'd like to know concerning the particulars of this case?''

Spunky, and cool when riled. Red hair definitely
a warning of some warmth in the temper zone.
''You don't like me asking you questions?''

''I don't mind you asking questions,'' she said,
passing him. ''I mind you questioning me in that
detached-cop voice, like you're recording data.
These babies aren't data, Ex-Officer McCallum.
They were left in my care, and like your father, I
have a vested interest in seeing that they are treated
with the utmost devotion.''

A fierce guardian she apparently planned to be.
''I would guess Ms. Barrows chose pretty well when
she picked you for surrogate mother.''

''I didn't ask to be the stand-in mother to these
children. But until *Jenny* is found, I plan on doing
as she asked.''

She returned to the nursery, keeping her back to
him as she ministered to the infants. He shifted uncomfortably. White pants trimmed a tiny little tush–
the woman was made like a doll. Even her shoulder
blade-length curls seemed like doll dross.

Well, he couldn't stand here and stare at her posterior all day. She'd clearly noted the lack of warmth
in his soul when it came to children, so it was best
to move along.

But then the devil seized him, and he tapped on

the window. She turned, clearly aware that it was him by the raised eyebrow she shot him as she neared the glass.

"Coffee at 2 p.m.?" he asked.

"Help yourself. The cafeteria's open then."

But he saw the challenge in her gaze, and he knew she'd be there.

Because she wanted Jenny Barrows found. And she'd made her point clear about the human element being the key to finding a scared young girl.

He really admired April Sullivan's grit.

APRIL LEFT CALEB sitting in the cafeteria for ten minutes past two o'clock before she slid a doughnut over his shoulder onto the table in front of him. "I heard police officers love doughnuts. This one might be a bit stale."

He fake-frowned at her as she took the plastic chair across from him. "You didn't see the sign that says, 'Don't feed the cops'?"

"But you're ex, right? So I'm free to ignore the sign."

"I couldn't help noticing the sign you're wearing says, 'Questions can be directed to the appropriate department, but not necessarily answered. And all in my own good time.'"

"Glad you can read." She popped open a soda can. "I'll do anything I can to help find Jenny, but I don't want to be questioned by RoboCop."

"I got it, I got it. There *is* a heart behind my bulletproof vest."

She gave him a stern eyeing, noting that his chest was broad, but not thick enough that he was wearing a vest. "Do you wear one as a security consultant?"

"Not usually. If I'm on the golf course with Dad, maybe."

That earned him a smile. "Now you're sounding more human."

"So, do you have any idea why Ms. Barrows— sorry, *Jenny*—might have disappeared like she did? And left those adorable bundles of joy to a virtual stranger?"

April drank some of her cola before answering. "Believe me, in the last several days, I've tried to put myself in Jenny's shoes. She was too young to be a mother, really, and certainly to quadruplets. Seventeen, widowed, her husband killed in a construction accident, no family support..." She shrugged. "It was a lot for her to handle, without even mentioning the stress of finding out what all had to happen to care for quads."

"If she doesn't return or isn't found, the children will go into foster care."

April froze. "Not if I have anything to do with it, they won't. Not for one damn minute."

"Hey, it's okay—"

"Not to me, it isn't. I don't even want to think about Jenny not returning. For goodness' sakes, she needs medical care herself! Surely one weak girl can be found. And these children deserve a true home."

"What's your beef with foster care?"

She bristled. "I simply…would not want that, considering that Jenny entrusted her children to me. A home isn't a home unless it's built on love, and a family isn't a family unless it's based on love. The babies should be ready to go home in a month. In that time, a lot can happen, like the mother being found by you, if Austin's finest can't do it. Isn't that why your father sent you? He wouldn't want them to go into foster care, either."

"Hey," he said, gently putting his hand over hers. "Chill, lady. I didn't mean to get you all upset. I'm beginning to think maybe you don't like me too much, kind of like oil and vinegar naturally repel each other."

She snatched her hand from under his. "It's good on some things."

"But it has to be shook real hard to stay together, and even that's not for long. Let's me and you work together on this without a lot of shaking, okay?"

"I don't want to talk about the babies going into foster care," she said stubbornly. "I want you to say you'll do your best to assist the officers and everyone else who's looking to find Jenny, since that's why you're here."

"You've got a lot in common with my dad."

His grim tone caught her ear, but she didn't heed it. "The man dedicated a wing to helping children and mothers who need extra attention. If you're putting me in the same category with him, I call that a good thing.''

He sighed, looking at her with some admiration. ''Beneath that delicate appearance, you're wearing steel determination, lady.''

''What would you do in my place? If you'd been left a heartbreaking note asking you to take care of someone's children?''

''I'd be scared as hell, if you want to know the truth.''

''Well, I am, Mr. Troubleshooter. I'm scared. I want to see the happy ending to this fairy tale right this minute.''

She stared at him to see how he was taking her brave words. But she wasn't exaggerating. She was frightened out of her wits, for Jenny's sake. The babies were fine, loved and stroked by everyone who was admitted to the neonatal nursery. But Jenny might be in pain, and she was most certainly frightened to have left the way she had. She had no money, nothing of value. She could be putting herself in danger, and the thought of it was more than April could bear.

Caleb looked at her, his hazel eyes dark with compassion and empathy. Okay, maybe he wasn't all data-seeking ex-cop. He was tall and well filled out, no doubt in shape from his days on the force. She suspected his story would be a tale of heartache, because he didn't strike her as an easy quitter. Witness how he'd overridden her cold shoulder and enticed her into a coffee break. "Are you going to eat that doughnut or not?"

He shoved it toward her. "You want it?"

"Never touch them. I watch my fat grams carefully."

That brought a laugh from him. "Why? Afraid to weigh more than ninety pounds?"

"I'm afraid to coagulate my bloodstream and arteries with sludge when I work twelve-hour shifts. And I weigh a very healthy one hundred five, thank you."

She stood, and he did, too.

"Then I'll pass on it as well." He tossed the doughnut into a nearby trash can. "Since I'll be working around the clock to find the missing mother of those babies."

"Thank you," she said quietly. "I would appreciate anything you could do. Not that I don't think the police won't find her eventually. But they have lots of cases and I'm afraid, Caleb. It's been nearly a week since anyone has heard anything."

She looked up at him, unwilling to think that maybe Jenny wouldn't be found, especially if she didn't want to be. The girl wouldn't have credit cards which would leave a paper trail. No family she might run to.

"Do you know anything at all about the husband?" Caleb asked. "Did either of them have family?"

"No. They were both orphans. She was living with a grandmotherly type named Mrs. Fox whom she mentioned from time to time. But the police have already checked with her, and Mrs. Fox had no more information than I do."

"There's got to be a school she attended."

"She'd dropped out," April said sadly. "Her husband as well, since he had to work to support them both. Jenny couldn't work because of the difficulty of a multiple-birth pregnancy."

"Okay. I'll check the buses and the airlines, though I don't guess she would have had money to get anywhere. And I'll check the teenage hot spots, in case anyone has seen her."

"You don't think she might have left town, do you?" April was horrified by the thought.

"Anything's possible."

Upset, April turned to go, then slowly returned her gaze to his. "I was in foster care," she said softly.

"Tell me something I couldn't figure out on my own," he replied gently. "Can you give me a description of Jenny which includes weight and height?"

She blinked back sudden tears. *Jenny, come back!* she thought. *These little lives need their mother. They need more than being broken up and shuttled through the cracks in the system.* "I'll have that description waiting at the nurses' desk when you're through eating,'' she said, hurrying away from the cafeteria.

It would be so unfair, so cruel if that's what happened. April just had to put her faith in the police force.

And if not them, then Caleb McCallum, troubleshooter and ex-cop, would have to be her knight in shining armor. He was a bit scarred. He didn't hang out with his family much—until Briana's surprise pregnancy, his sister didn't hear all that often from him. She knew that from her close relationship with Bri; she was aware of the family tree.

She also knew that since Briana's babies had arrived, Caleb had thought up one excuse or another to visit her house.

Now that April had finally met the big bad ex-cop, she decided he was a man who didn't want his bluff called. He wanted to act as if he didn't care about these quadruplets—but he did.

She wouldn't call his bluff on that matter. But she wouldn't allow him to underestimate her, either.

IT WASN'T THAT he minded his job as a security consultant, Caleb thought as he waited at the nurse's desk for April to give him the weight/height description of Jenny. What bugged him was being called in on family matters, with his dad's constant reminders of his past. Maybe his dad wanted to live in his grief by building a monument to it—the birth wing—but Caleb preferred to let time heal his wounds. If time, in fact, could do that.

Since the death of his close friend and cop partner a few years ago, Caleb was pretty certain time had slowed to a crawl.

It was either his dad's disbelief that his son would never return to the force, or perhaps Jackson's desire to remind Caleb that time *was* passing him that made him keep asking him to "use his contacts" about matters that concerned babies.

Okay, when his unmarried sister, Bri, had become pregnant with triplets, Caleb hadn't needed too damn much convincing to want to find the father. He'd very much felt that he would use all his contacts, and every bit of cop determination he'd ever possessed to find the guy and explain to him how much he *really* wanted to be married to his sister.

Bri, ever independent, had stayed his search. That situation had resolved itself fine.

Maybe this one would, too. On the other hand, he had to admit a strong desire to see the case closed with a happy ending. It sure would upset April Sullivan if those babies were taken by the state. Goose pimples ran over his hands at the thought. What a feminine little woman! When his father had asked him to look in on this case, he could have had no idea about the compact bundle of steely determination he would meet up with.

Caleb frowned. And then again, Jackson had been dropping hints for some time about Caleb needing a woman to help him through the rough time in his life. Romance. A wife.

That was the last thing he wanted. A wife should be a partner, and he didn't want any more partners. He didn't want to get close to anyone; he didn't want to feel responsibility for a single soul. Take April, for example. Now, she'd suck up a lot of attention. For one thing, he'd sensed she had emotional baggage a lot like his. Clearly, she was a woman with a lot of weather, and while he liked a storm or two, he also wanted calm more than anything these days. And she was so *fragile.* Those tiny bones in her hand had instantly made him relax his handshake to the point that he'd almost been holding her hand rather than sharing a greeting. It had been like palming warm satin.

He bet those hands felt good to those tiny infants. From pictures, he'd seen that his mother was a fragile flower compared to his father's hearty stature and—

Oh, no. No, no, no. He was the youngest triplet, the one his mother had brought last into the world. The scrawny one. Yet, might she have lived had there been one less child? What made one woman bear four infants and be strong enough to run away, and another woman unable to withstand the arduous process of birthing three? He wasn't certain, but it might have something to do with constitution and frame, and April, while she had tugged on his male instincts, was a big red stop sign. Well, a petite red stop sign, but a woman he wasn't going to allow to get under his skin. He definitely didn't need a dainty flower that couldn't withstand the rigors of his roughhouse cop personality.

"Here's a description of Jenny," April said, handing him a slip of paper. "All the pertinent details."

Starting, he found himself looking into her deep green eyes. Eyes that looked at him no-nonsense, as if she fully expected him to walk out into the street and come back inside the hospital, producing Jenny Barrows in all of ten minutes.

"Social Services called a moment ago," she told him. "They plan to come by today to begin overseeing their role with the children. For now, these babies are too frail to leave the hospital, but in a month, maybe sooner, that won't be the situation. If Jenny isn't found, I fully intend to do everything I can to make certain I comply with her wish that I raise the babies."

He cocked an eyebrow at the determined diminutive redhead. "How are you going to do that? Raise four babies by yourself? You'll have to quit your job."

"I am prepared to do whatever it takes, Mr. McCallum."

Waving a hand in surrender, he said, "Caleb. Don't go all formal on me again. I'm on your side, all right? I'm just asking you how you're going to do it."

"How could I *not* do it?"

"Okay, okay. Do you have a boyfriend, or some-one who can help you?"

She put a hand on her hip. "If you want to know my status, why don't you just ask me rather than phony-baloneying about it?"

Whoa, she was a Tartar. What she lacked in size, she definitely had in spirit. He tucked the informa-tion she'd given him into his pocket. "I'm just try-ing to determine if you have any resources that might make Social Services look favorably upon you as a temporary mother."

"I'm a nurse trained in neonatal intensive care. I was the one Jenny Barrows turned to. And I want to do it. I'm not afraid of a challenge. Other tem-porary-care situations will split the babies up."

"All right, April. You let me know if you hear anything. This is my cell number," he said, scrib-bling on a piece of paper and handing it to her. "It's always on. I'll let you know if I find out anything the police haven't been able to turn up themselves."

"I hope you're better at asking questions with other people than you've shown yourself to be with me." She raised an eyebrow at him.

Oh, brother. She just wasn't going to leave it alone, because she'd squarely caught him trying to figure out if she was unattached, and she knew it. Denial wasn't going to work here; she was too smart for that. But a man had his pride. He frowned at her and said, "You're entitled to your opinion, Miss Sullivan."

She laughed at him, not fooled for a second, then turned around and walked to the other side of the nurse's desk, giving him a view of that sweetheart-shaped tush in action.

And then she glanced over her shoulder, dead-on catching him staring at her fanny.

Oh, brother.

Chapter Two

"You didn't answer my question," he said.

"It didn't merit an answer. Social Services will consider my skills and other matters as a single mother, I hope, if it comes to that. You find Jenny, and I'll focus on spiffing up my foster parent qualifications in case you don't locate her in time. But I fully intend to do what I can for the children," she replied, disappearing into a hospital room.

It was an empty room, which was good, because she needed to collect her thoughts. Her words were almost all bravado. Even she knew that she might be an unlikely candidate because of her marital status. Possibly even a married couple might not be allowed to take in all four children.

The best thing for these children would be for Jenny to come back today. But if Jenny didn't return, and Social Services didn't look favorably upon her request to take them, they would be split up and put into varying foster care situations.

The thought was enough to tear April's heart in

two. It wasn't that her adoptive family hadn't loved her—they had. Yet all the years of being moved from one home to another had taken its toll. Friends, schools, addresses—nothing ever stayed the same. No relationship ever cemented for her, and she'd grown wary of trying to build any relationship in her life.

In fact, she'd learned to simply rely upon herself. By the time she was adopted, she was a teenager. While appreciative of her new mother and father, she'd almost felt as if she were adopted to take care of them. That wasn't fair, because they loved her to this day. They'd seen she was put through college and then nursing school, and that she had everything she needed.

But the foundation of love she'd lacked all her childhood couldn't be filled in. Independence became her sole weapon against pain; any friends she maintained knew that although she was kind and loving, she could be bullheaded about staying whatever course she chose without allowing anyone to help her.

That's why Caleb McCallum sent prickles of panic running all through her. While she'd recognized that this unexpected source of assistance might be beneficial if Jenny could be located for her children, she'd also perceived a strength and determination in Caleb congruent to her own.

Strong men always seemed to want to take care

of her—and then they were disappointed when she wouldn't allow that to happen.

While knowing that Caleb's personality was equal to hers, she also had to admit to feeling a thrill that he found her attractive. Sometimes, she spent so much time in a nurse's uniform that she forgot that she was a woman with a feminine wish to be attractive.

Caleb's gaze had told her she was—and so, for the moment, she could almost forgive him for trying to figure out her relationship status, a point she didn't want to dwell on because he'd been right about Social Services favoring married couples. She smiled to herself. He'd fished so badly that she almost found it cute—almost.

Poking her head into the hallway, she saw that it was devoid of the big, strong ex-officer and hospital personnel, so she slipped into the nursery for a last stroke for the babies before she went home. Each lay sleeping, with either a fist or a finger in their mouths. "I'll be so glad when these tubes come off," she told them softly. "And I'll be even happier when you have healthy birth weights."

They'd been alive so short a time. Four flannel wrapped responsibilities in cocoons of warm softness, blissfully unaware of the turmoil their mother's disappearance was causing. Caleb hadn't wanted to see them as anything more than an impersonal case his father had tossed at him. "It's going to be okay," she murmured, reaching in through the rubber-glove opening to touch the smallest baby's foot. "What you children need, I think, is to be called something other than babies one, two, three and four. Since you're supposed to be mine, why don't we think up some names, temporarily at least? Then maybe everyone will see that you're real little people, not numbers."

They didn't move, too content for the moment, but this would change soon enough. As soon as one awakened, usually all of them would begin flailing tiny fists and feet. "You're the big sister," she said to the baby in the first isolette. "You can be Melissa. When I was a little girl, I was in a home with a girl whom I desperately wanted to become my big sister. Her name was Melissa, and I remember her telling me that her name meant bee in Greek."

Picking up a pen, she wrote Melissa on the card attached to the front of the isolette. Then she reached for a baby names book. "Let's call you Chloe," she told the second pink-wrapped girl, "because it's pretty. And according to this book, it means blooming. I guess every bee needs a bloom, huh?"

She chuckled to herself. "Number three, lucky number three. A man should have a strong name, right?" Caleb was a strong name, as was Jackson. "But I don't want you to be so strong that you're tough and unreachable," she told the tiny boy. "Yet I believe that comes from nurture not nature." Frowning, she thought about what she knew about Caleb. Bri had said once that Caleb was the sibling who didn't really fit in somehow. They loved him, but many times he wantcd to be alone, choosing a harder path for himself than any his two siblings took. If they went hiking at summer camp, he had to go over the rocks to get where they were going, while they took the marked trails.

"Craig," she whispered to the baby. "It means crag. And we'll take care of the nurture thing so that you don't grow up too tough and unreachable. A little is good, too much is…well, it means a lonely path for you. And now you," she said to the last, smallest baby. "You need a special name. I'll call you…Matthew. Did you know that means gift of God? Well, it does, according to this handy-dandy book."

Closing the names book, she finished writing all the names on the cards. Satisfied for the moment that she'd given the babies a reason to become real people and not just numbers to even the most stalwart of tough hearts, she went to sign off her shift.

Slipping her hand into her pocket, she felt the note that had changed her life. Pulling it out, she read the note for the hundredth time:

Dear April Sullivan,
I know you'll love my babies and take good care of them, so I want you to have them.
                                    Jenny Barrows

The words, written in immature lettering on a piece of school notebook paper, cried out the young teenager's despair. *She had to have been so desperate to appoint a near stranger as the guardian to her precious babies!* April was twenty-seven, and she knew she'd feel overwhelmed by the thought of raising four tiny infants alone, as precious as they might be. But she would do it.

Replacing the note in her pocket, she headed to the nurses' station. To her dismay, a Social Services worker was at the desk, speaking to the head neonatal nurse, Cherilyn Connors.

"April, this is Mandy Cole from Social Services. April Sullivan is the nurse to whom Jenny left the note concerning her children."

"How do you do?" Mandy said.

April looked the tall brunette over without trying to seem obvious. "I'm fine, thank you," she said carefully, wondering if the woman would be sympathetic to her plea for temporary custody.

"I'm going to examine the infants," Mandy said. "Is there anything you feel I should know about them?"

The question was directed to either Cherilyn or April, she noted. But it was April who wanted answers. "We can go over their files together, if you'd like. What will you do after you examine them?"

"We'll continue to monitor them. If Ms. Barrows doesn't return, or if the children become healthy enough to leave, they'll be placed in temporary care until the situation can be resolved more satisfactorily.''

Misgiving rose inside April. ''Jenny's wish is that I take care of her children. I am willing to do so.''

Mandy looked at her with some surprise. ''The paper Ms. Barrows left itself is not a legal document. I'm certain you realize the difference, Ms. Sullivan, between a legal document and an emotionally distraught young girl's note?''

''I recognize this, Ms. Cole, but I also am willing to take the emotionally distraught young girl's wishes into consideration.''

''May I ask how old you are?'' Mandy asked. ''I see that this particular wing is new. How long have you been employed as a nurse, here or anywhere else? And are you married, Ms. Sullivan? This is information germane to any application you might wish to put forward.''

With those words, April realized Caleb had been right. Regardless of what Jenny had wanted, or what she, April, might be willing to do for those sweet babies, she would not be considered as a temporary foster mother.

And that meant the babies would go into the system.

CALEB HAD RETURNED to the hospital, after going down to the nearby Austin police station to talk to some guys he knew who would give up the information on the missing mom, when a small dynamo swept past him, walking fast toward the parking lot. "Hey," he said, reaching out to grab April's arm gently. "Going somewhere? Remember me?"

She kept her head down, and he realized she was upset. "Hello, what's going on?" he asked, encircling her with one arm. "Are you okay, April? Did something happen?"

She shook her head, a sniffle escaping her as she blew her nose into a tissue. Despite the parking-lot lights, it was too dark outside for him to see her face, but clearly, the calm tigress of a lady had some unexpected troubles.

"Ah," he said soothingly, tugging her up against his chest. "Didn't you know it's okay to talk to police officers? Police officers are our friends," he said in a singsong teacher's voice.

Though she didn't laugh at his attempt to cheer her, she didn't pull away from his chest. He decided to shut up and go with the physical comfort, because one, it was working, and two, she felt good. Underneath the nurse's smock, delicate shoulder blades quivered. And man alive, was her waist ever tiny.

"You were right. Social Services isn't even going to remotely consider me as a temporary mother for the babies. You've just got to find Jenny somehow!" she finally cried on a wail.

He felt a little better now that he knew the issue they were confronting. "No single moms, huh?"

"No single, young, barely-out-of-nursing-school

moms allowed. Scraps of paper are not legal documents, and don't you forget it.''

"Whew. You didn't enjoy that conversation, and I think I understand why.''

"Well,'' April said, finally moving away from the shelter he'd tried to give her. "I understand her point. Social Services has a job to do, and they do it under sometimes impossible situations, and always highly emotional ones. I was just hoping so much that, in this case, they'd allow me some leeway.''

"Not a chance?''

"Not a chance.''

He moved his fingers down to her elbow. "Let me walk you to your car.''

Nodding, she began walking the way she'd been going when he'd stopped her. He let his hand fall away from her, just keeping up easily with her quick pace. "Did you know that Jenny was actually a good student?''

She stopped abruptly, swiveling to stare up at him. "No, I didn't. How do you know?''

"Because I've been doing my job. She was a better-than-good student. According to some of my buddies who did the initial interviews of the hospital staff and the landlady when Jenny first went missing, the teenager was a remarkable student, as was her husband. They felt a need to prove themselves. Apparently, their relationship was for real, and they expected to get married and go on to college, where they could live in married-student housing, work, and rely on each other for emotional support. Finding themselves pregnant moved the timetable up, and they had to marry and drop out of high school. But these were not troublemaker kids.''

"No. Jenny didn't strike me as that type. But I would never have guessed that she had planned to go to college.''

"Mrs. Fox told the police that both David—the deceased husband—and Jenny planned to get their GED, and they had both applied to the same colleges, also with applications for student aid. They were sincere in their efforts, and they meant to make it happen. After David died a few months ago and Jenny moved in with Mrs. Fox, Jenny began to become uncertain as to whether she would even try to attend a local college. The babies, of course, would need every minute of her time for the first several years. But without income, Jenny knew she'd have to work at a minimum-wage job. All this stress began weighing on her. She mentioned several times that she wished she could give the babies the home they deserved.''

April stood still, looking at him.

"She must have seen an awful lot of good in you,'' he said softly, "to decide that you were just the answer to her prayers.''

April shook her head. "She was desperate. I don't think Jenny knew what she was doing. After giving birth, many women suffer postpartum blues. With

Jenny, this would have been doubly manifest, I believe, because of the grief she was already suffering from losing her husband.''

''Maybe. But I now have to look at it from a different angle, based on this information,'' he told her. ''You're saying she was grief-stricken, and once she comes to her senses, will return. I'm saying, yes, she was grief-stricken, but moreover, she desperately wanted her children to have everything she couldn't give them. She met you, saw a kindred spirit who had made it where she had once dreamed to go, and she knew you'd love her children. Like a dying mother who fights to the last instant to create the best world she can for her offspring, Jenny gave you to her babies.''

''Rather than giving her babies to me.''

''Right. You were the gift, the way of a better life. I believe Jenny has no plans whatsoever to return. None.''

Chapter Three

April could hardly take Caleb's words in—and yet, there was a core of logic she couldn't ignore. "I would never, ever have thought what you just said."

"Because you're going from the perspective of empathy," he said. "In an optimum world—yours—the mother is tired and frightened and will return once her medical condition, the blues exaggerated by grief, is overridden by the love for her children. But Jenny's world was far from optimum. Though I don't believe she thought her actions through with any sense of clarity or comprehension, I believe she was acting on the survival-of-the-fittest theory. Because she was desperate, and she was fighting for her children's survival."

"You know, you're very good at this," April said slowly. "You were an awesome cop, weren't you?"

He raised an eyebrow at her. "Now who's asking bad questions? Let's get you to your car and get you home. You look like you could fall asleep on your feet."

April ignored his guiding hand as she thought through the picture he'd drawn. "So what you're saying is that you feel Jenny didn't know that her children would be split up and put into foster care."

"I am positive that, while she was book smart, she was quite innocent about how the system works," Caleb said. "She'd gotten pregnant, which, in hers and David's history of being orphans themselves, they would have most likely been eager to avoid. While many teens get pregnant because they're bored, or they're subconsciously wanting someone to love them, David and Jenny were not bored. They were working toward a common goal. And they didn't need anyone to feel loved by, per se, because they had each other. I'd bet the pregnancy was a total accident. You see that it changed their plans, and therefore, their lives, forever."

"Being unsophisticated about birth control doesn't mean Jenny was unsophisticated about what might happen to her babies if she abandoned them. She watches TV like any other teenager."

"But," Caleb said, tugging April forward so he could take her to her car, "she chose her replacement. Would she have known that Social Services wouldn't heed her request? *You* seemed to think her wishes might make a difference. You told me you're willing to take those babies. Jenny probably felt that your bond with the babies and your training might make a difference." He paused for a moment, then said, "You are determined, and you are capable, and

Jenny no doubt sensed you'd do your best to stand up for her children's rights. What she didn't know is that she has to sign a legal document giving up all rights to her children before you could ever adopt them legally. They can't be adopted by anyone until the living mother authorizes adoption.''

April's heart stilled inside her. "So although Jenny meant to provide for her newborns, she's actually put them in the very situation she grew up in herself. Orphaned. Oh my God." April couldn't help the tears that swept down her face all over again.

"Here, here," Caleb said, pulling her into his embrace again. "Crying's not going to help, April."

But she was shaking and she couldn't stop, so for once she allowed herself to take comfort from someone else. *Just for this moment, I need Caleb. I'll cry it all out, and then I'll be strong again.*

"You're too upset to drive. Let me take you home. Come on," he said, trying to move her.

She shook her head against his chest, but he was adamant. "I'm at least going to follow you home to make certain you get there safely, so you might as well give in gracefully."

"I don't think I know how to give in gracefully," she mumbled, wiping her nose on a tissue she jerked from her purse.

"Now, why does that not surprise me? Miss Chock-Full-of-Spit-and-Fire doesn't give in gracefully. Surprise, surprise."

She laughed reluctantly through her tears. "I don't think I like you when you're being sarcastic."

He snorted. "That doesn't bode well for our working relationship. I like to be sarcastic sometimes. It keeps me from getting bowled over emotionally by little red-haired women who wail all over my big strong chest."

"Oh, please!" But that brought the smile to her face he'd been trying to find, so she decided just this once she would give in gracefully and let Caleb follow her home.

"I guess you're going to want coffee or a nightcap when we get to my house."

"After that nasty doughnut you tried to give me earlier, I may be too frightened to take anything else from you. But I deserve a nightcap after all the thinking I've done today. It's not easy running lithely through the trails of the teenage feminine brain."

She suspected it was very easy for him, and was even more convinced that seeing different angles in every situation had made him a damn fine cop. Never would she have seen Jenny's dilemma the way he had.

"I warn you that the trails of the feminine brain are tricky at any age," she teased. "Do you still want to join me for a nightcap?"

"I'm on duty until the case is solved, aren't I? If you've got orange juice, I'll take you up on it."

"That I have." She dug in her purse for her keys.

"Bri did tell me once that women fell for you like mad, and that you rarely noticed it happening. She said you were an accidental seducer." She raised an eyebrow at him. "I'm inviting you in for orange juice, but please, do not think I can be accidentally seduced or otherwise."

He laughed, not offended. "My big sister has a head full of romantic rocks. Ignore her."

"One should never ignore their best friend."

"Well, if anyone is safe with me, it's you, babe. Come on. Let's get you home."

What the heck did he mean by that? She turned quickly before he could see that his casual statement had unsettled her.

Much more than she wanted to admit.

"WE NEED a plan B," April told him once they'd stepped inside her house. Caleb hadn't been too shocked by the white compact car she drove—very clean and spare—and the house was what he would have expected as well, although something niggled at him, though he couldn't put his finger on it. Everything was in its tidy place, with delicate hues on the walls and in the carpet. The word he would have used to describe it was *dollhouse.*

"Plan B for what?" he asked, distracted by the lace drapes. In his apartment, he never bothered to open the plastic shutters. April's drapes hung like fairy-tale wisps, tied with soft blue bows. He scratched at the back of his neck, wondering if he was beginning to break out in a rash. Or hives.

"For making certain the babies aren't put in four separate homes. There has to be something we can do. We know for sure that Jenny didn't mean for that to happen."

"Did you sew your own drapes?" he asked, absently taking the glass of orange juice she handed him as he stood awkwardly in the living room.

"Of course." She laughed at him. "Why do you ask?"

His gaze roamed the kitchen she'd stepped from. Tiny vases sat in a collection atop a counter; china dishes were placed along the wall for ornamentation.

He swallowed uncomfortably. "If your toilet broke, what would you do about it?"

She looked at him as if he'd lost his mind. "I'd fix it, of course. What's hard about that? There's a ball and a chain and some plumbing. I laid the tile myself in the kitchen. One reads the directions, takes a do-it-yourself class at the local repair store and then goes home and puts the tile in. What are you really asking me?"

"When Jenny was in the hospital for those two weeks before she gave birth, did you talk about your house at all? Or sewing? Cooking? Woman things of that nature?"

Her forehead wrinkled up delightfully as she thought about his question. "Yes, I'm sure I did. What else was there to talk about? Before I'd go off duty for the days I wasn't scheduled, she'd ask me what I planned to do with my time. And so I told her. At the time, I believe I was working on a cross-stitch for your sister's nursery.''

He drained the juice and reached around her to put the glass on the counter. "Okay. Well, thanks for the libation. Guess I'd better let you get some rest.''

''Not until you tell me what you're thinking. You're working on something, and I want to hear what you've come up with, since I now realize you've been running through the trails of my brain.''

''Okay.'' He drew a deep breath. ''But don't go all ballistic on me.''

She shrugged. ''I can't make any promises. Hope you've got your flak jacket on.''

''I think you'd like a baby someday.''

She blew a raspberry. ''You can do better than that! You didn't have to stand here asking silly questions about toilet repair to say, 'Okay, she's a female, and females approaching their thirties want children ninety-five percent of the time.' ''

He held up his hands. ''But did you *know* you wanted a baby?''

There was no way she was going to share her dreams with him—not now. ''You're safe, Caleb, I promise you. Even if I did install my own tile floor.''

Brushing that aside, he said, ''And did you also

know you might have subconsciously projected your dreams very clearly to Jenny?''

APRIL HAD THOUGHT any number of things might happen if she allowed Caleb inside her house. Bri had mentioned that the opposite sex seemed terminally tempted by his loner appeal. Maybe she'd thought he'd make some attempt to hold her again. Quite possibly, that's why she had allowed him inside her home on the pretext of serving him a drink. She'd answered his questions about her home with a sense of pride.

Never had she thought he might be analyzing her. When he'd said she was safe with him—she hadn't known how safe.

''Caleb, if you're trying to say that I subconsciously told Jenny I wanted children—her children—I've got to tell you that you've gone way off the deep end.''

He sank into the sofa, uninvited. She could tell he was so deep in thought he didn't realize she was becoming angry. ''Could she have chosen you out of a sense of gratitude? Maybe even as a way to make your dreams come true? That would definitely lead me to conclude that she's not coming back, which would also mean that it would be good to start checking bus stations—''

''Caleb,'' April interrupted. ''Stop. I did not push my dreams onto Jenny. I did not position myself as the answer to her prayers. You're supposed to drink your orange juice, possibly murmur something nice about seeing me soon and then leave. Definitely you're not supposed to be conducting a case file on me.''

Surprise touched his face. ''April, I'm working all angles. You wanted me to find Jenny, didn't you? Well, when am I supposed to turn off the sensors?''

Feminine annoyance made her voice sharp. ''When you start checking me over as a suspect.''

''Not a suspect. An unsuspecting, maybe even unwilling, player in Jenny's desperation.''

She wasn't sure she was mollified, so she went into the kitchen for a few moments, examining whether she was upset because he just might have a point, or if she was miffed because she'd hoped he might try for a kiss before he left—and clearly had no intentions of that. She'd noticed he was tired, anyway. ''I'd better let you go. You probably need some sleep before your inner-cop clock runs past a twenty-four-hour shift.''

There was no answer, so she turned to see the expression on his face.

But the big, rough-and-tough man had fallen asleep, his head cradled on one of the soft ribbon pillows she'd made.

''Yo, dream man,'' she said, nearing him.

He gave a tiny snore of exhaustion.

Rolling her eyes, she got an afghan out of the closet. ''Your sister was wrong about you being terminally tempting to the opposite sex. And by the way, I crocheted this myself, you lummox." None too delicately, she tossed his booted feet up onto the sofa and dumped the afghan on him. "And I upholstered the sofa you're snoozing on, and I painted these walls myself, and I'll have you know, none of it was done with any thought of trying to snare you, so you can rest easy."

CALEB AWAKENED, bolting upright as he wondered if he'd heard a sound. It was dark; he was sitting on April's sofa. Touching a button on his watch, green numbers glowed the hour. It was 5:00 a.m.

It was the first time he'd spent the night in a woman's house in quite a while. But there had been no up-close-and-personal time before he'd snoozed. He wished he hadn't fallen asleep on her. *Scintillating conversationalist*—that's me. *Real impressive.* Reaching to a table beside the sofa, he flipped on the lamp. Two blankets covered him, put on him by April. He'd brought her home to comfort her and make certain she was all right. Their roles had reversed, and he found it an embarrassment to the macho bravado he'd been wearing around April.

Time to make himself scarce. But first, he decided to check on Nurse Sullivan. Just a glance, to make certain she was securely tucked into her bed.

Folding the blankets, he tossed them onto the sofa, then headed down a narrow hallway. He switched on a light, seeing that there were two empty bedrooms on the left, a sewing room on the right and a hall bathroom. At the end of the hall, there was a closed door—the only place she could be. Quietly, he reached out a hand and edged the door open, every sense sharp as he waited for his eyes to adjust.

A double bed centered the room, with white sheets, white bedspread, white pillows—too much, if you asked him. But in the center of the ethereal white, April lay sprawled, a tousled yet relaxed flame at rest. Her hair was flung over her pillow; one slender leg poked from covers that had twisted around her waist.

He felt heat rising inside him, and decided waking up with April could take the chill off of late-December mornings real fast. She looked like pure temptation to him.

Yet, the clear reminder of who April was lay clustered in every window, in every edge of free space on dressers and the window seat. Dolls of every nationality, type and material kept a gentle vigil of forever childhood, satisfied to watch over April's most vulnerable moments.

That vulnerability frightened him—and yet drew him inexorably to her bedside. He couldn't stop looking at her delicate skin, her lips as they curved in her sleep. The leg so frankly exposed made him nervous even as he couldn't take his gaze from her. So, to return the favor she'd provided him, he took hold of the white blanket she'd kicked to the foot of the bed and slowly pulled it up over her until he reached her neck.

He glanced at her face, instantly finding her eyes wide open and watching him.

"There for a minute I thought you were going to frisk me," she said, her voice husky with sleep.

"Well, if you want me to—"

"Mr. Troubleshooter, I think you missed your chance last night."

Her smile robbed him of the ability to decide if she was lodging a complaint or not. "I apologize for falling asleep. I'm usually better company than that."

She sat up against the pillows, keeping the blanket tight to her. "I wouldn't know."

"Oh, come on. You do know. You like me, in some way."

"Maybe. Not when you're yelling in your sleep, though. That gave me the heebie-jeebies." Auburn eyebrows rose over concerned eyes. "Do you do that often? Because if you do, I'm going to send some dolls home with you to chase away the monsters in your mind."

He sent a glance around her room. "Does it work?"

"In lieu of pets, they're less bother, cost, and my work schedule suits them. Sure. They're great company. Take a few with you. Or ten. If you have those doozy nightmares often."

Swallowing, he tried to forget about the dainty

body beneath the sheets. He'd noticed she wore only a short, pink T-shirt and some pajama shorts. Not enough to tame his libido, and in fact, keeping his brain busy with electrified hormones. "Believe it or not, I slept better than I have in a long time."

"Really? On a sofa, in your jeans and boots." Her eyes twinkled at him.

"Well, no doubt I could have slept better in here—"

"And that's my cue to say grab a glass of orange juice from the fridge and show yourself out," April said with a smile. "I'm sure you need to get back on the case."

"Do you have to work today?"

"No. But I will go in to see the babies." At that thought, her shy smile disappeared.

"Don't think about it," he said quickly. "Either Jenny will be found, or...or—"

"Or not. And as I mentioned last night, I need a plan B."

"Are you losing faith in me?"

She shook her head at him, her gaze solemn. "Just the system."

He grunted. "You only have your marital status and age mainly working against you, right? Not insurmountable odds. Unless it's Social Services you're pitted against. But they do have a job to do, under thankless circumstances."

"I know. But there isn't a doubt in my mind that, unless Jenny returns, I can provide those babies with much of what they need for a balanced and happy life.''

Glancing around the dolls keeping silent watch, he nodded. ''You don't have to convince me that you, better than anyone, maybe understand the odds those children are up against.''

''And I love them.''

''And you love them.'' There wasn't a doubt in his mind about that. He'd seen how she lingered over each baby's bassinet, tenderly touching them. *It's all wrong. Too many children get left behind in a system that means well. They should have a mother. It's not that April is the only woman who would love these babies, but she already does.*

April is already their mother.

The phone rang, startling both of them in the cold morning light illuminating her room. April picked up the phone by her bed. ''Hello?''

She listened for a few moments, and as he watched panic stretch its shadow over April's face, Caleb felt his gut tighten with apprehension.

Chapter Four

"Baby Matthew's missing," April told Caleb, jumping out of bed and trying to keep the view of white, freckle-spattered skin to a minimum as she snatched on a green terry-cloth robe. Caleb may have appointed himself her one-night guardian, but she didn't know him well enough to forgo modesty. "I'm going to have to get down to the hospital. I hate to toss you out, but—"

"Wait. Who is Baby Matthew?" Caleb demanded.

Frantically, she pulled her hair up into a knot as she hurried into her closet. "Baby Barrows number four, the littlest of the babies," she called. "I named him Matthew."

"How can he be missing?"

"I don't know! I didn't stop to ask the particulars. If Cherilyn calls me at five in the a.m. to tell me he's missing, I can assure you it's not bad hospital humor."

"How can that happen? The baby had tubes in him."

"I don't know." Her heart was beating almost too hard for her to think clearly. "I can't think about that right now. I just want to get there."

"I'll drive you to the hospital."

"I'm okay." She didn't know if she wanted to continue allowing this man to look out for her. He was definitely trying to be caring, but independence was a hard habit to break. "No, thanks. I'll probably stay at the hospital all day with the babies, anyway."

Having fully dressed in the walk-in closet, April grabbed a coat, stuffing her arms into it as she looked at Caleb. His stance was stiff, as if he didn't quite know what to do with himself. "I don't want to start leaning on you. You're a nice man, but I've gotten used to taking care of myself."

"I know." He nodded his understanding. "We'll skip over the fact that you're upset and it would be better if you weren't driving. I'll follow you, and if you do anything vehicularly heinous—like drive eighty in a fifty-five—I'll honk the horn. Just in case you miss the speed limit signs or something."

"How can one tiny baby be lost?" she fretted, pulling on walking boots, not even registering his effort to keep the situation light. "He was too fragile to go anywhere. And surely no one would remove his tubes to slip him out."

"Let's just get down there and find out what's

happening. It doesn't do any good to envision scenarios. The police will have been called, and probably soon the media will be, too.''

They left the house, April locking the door and hurrying to her car. Caleb followed in his—and the sight of his car behind her gave her some measure of reassurance.

CALEB COULD HARDLY believe that someone would take a tiny baby, especially under the watchful eyes of so much hospital personnel, but the grim expression on the head nurse's face told the story.

"The quads are never alone," she told him. "There is always supposed to be at least one nurse inside the neonatal care room. They are special needs babies, requiring constant care, especially as not all problems show up immediately after birth. Early this morning, we were short on personnel, and the nurse stepped out to retrieve something—which took only moments—and when she returned, the isolette with Baby Barrows number four was gone.''

"Matthew," he murmured. "Someone rolling an isolette couldn't have gotten far without being seen.''

Annabelle Reardon, a delivery nurse, spoke up. "We immediately had security posted at every exit we could cover. Unfortunately, at the hour that this occurred there are not many patients awake, and the hospital crews are a bit more understaffed. Particularly in this new wing, there are many empty rooms where someone could have hidden until they saw the hall was clear.''

"Someone knows something." Caleb thought about April, down in the nursery with the remaining three babies. She'd told him she'd watch over the infants, and he could investigate this latest turn of events. He admired that she came in focused and ready to do her part, and leave the searching to him and the officers on duty. She could have been frantic—which he knew she was, but trying to keep her panic at bay—and his attention would have been divided between Matthew's disappearance and her fear. "My first thought is that a patient took the baby," he told Annabelle and Cherilyn.

"We have no one we're caring for at this time. Just those four Barrows babies," Cherilyn told him.

"In the main hospital, where the regular deliveries take place, there are many patients, though," Annabelle said.

"How do we find out if anyone recently had a pregnancy that might have ended unsatisfactorily?" Caleb asked.

"As in a stillbirth?" Annabelle asked.

"Possibly."

"Well, the records of births are in the computer. To my knowledge, only one stillbirth occurred, and that was a week ago. A Mrs. Cannady, first child."

"Okay," Caleb said. "Let's start by having every single room of the main hospital searched. I'll check these rooms, although I don't think the kidnapper is here.''

"You don't think someone would harm baby Matthew?" Cherilyn asked.

"No. I believe that someone heard about these quads on the news, and knows that the mother is missing. My guess is that someone desperately wants a child, and is figuring that here are four no one wants. She may even feel like she is doing Matthew a favor by keeping him from a life of foster care.'' He knew how apprehensive April was about foster care.

"I heard one of the officers say they needed to question April about this,'' Cherilyn said worriedly.

"Not a chance," Caleb said. "I might have thought the same thing, knowing April's fear of the system. However, I went home with her last night, and know for a fact she slept all night.''

"Oh-h-h,'' Annabelle and Cherilyn said together.

He shook his head. "Not the way it sounds.''

"I suppose we should have known that,'' Annabelle said with a sigh. "Knowing April the way we do. Oh, well.''

They looked upon him so pityingly that Caleb realized they felt sorry for him, as if April had chewed him up and spat him out as date material.

"It's not quite that way, either. I was concerned about her and told her I was going to follow her home. She invited me in for a glass of orange juice, and I fell asleep on her sofa, where she tossed a couple of blankets over me and—'' He suddenly remembered the sensation of warmth covering him. For all the nights he couldn't sleep through the night, that gentle warmth had lulled him right back. April had covered him, not once, but twice.

''You were saying, Caleb?'' Cherilyn prodded. ''You fell asleep?''

He realized they were having some fun at his expense, but that was all right. ''The details aren't important. Let's just leave it at the fact that Matthew isn't hidden in April's house, as much as she might like to have him. All of them.''

Cherilyn shook her head. ''I'd like to see that happen as well. But Social Services let her know fairly plainly that a one-parent family wouldn't be considered.''

''I know.'' He nodded to both women. ''I'm going to go check on her.''

''Good idea,'' Annabelle said. ''She doesn't know it, but she needs someone to think of her, at least until this is all over.''

April hadn't let him do anything for her. In fact, *she'd* cared for him. There wasn't any way he could think of to get her to lean on him. Yet, everyone needed someone they could shift some emotional weight to from time to time.

He shifted his emotional weight to…no. No one, anymore. Once upon a time, Terry Jakes had been his partner. But now…he kept his emotions solely under wraps.

Walking to the nursery, he'd found April exactly where he knew she'd be. "April," he said softly, tapping against the glass to get her attention.

She looked up, put down the towel she was folding and came into the hall. "Hi."

"I shouldn't have said that you might have projected your dreams onto Jenny so that she began to see you as someone she could gift with her children. I'm sorry. When I'm thinking through angles, I let my mind go pretty much."

"Your mind was definitely gone at that point," April said wryly. "I didn't pay any attention to that nonsense you were spouting. Any man who falls asleep on my sofa after exercising his brain to that extent deserves a stiff back and a sore neck." Her eyes suddenly darkened. "Do you think Jenny came back?"

"And what? Stole her own son? For what purpose?"

"Well, I don't know. If I ascribe any reality to your nonsense, maybe she would take one and leave me three."

"Nah." He shook his head. "She wouldn't take the littlest one. Jenny had strong survival instincts in her for her children, or she wouldn't have left them to you. She's not back, much as I wish she was."

"Then where is Matthew?" April demanded, her voice high and shrill, almost a wail as she started weeping. "He needs to be in there with his brother and sisters, where I can make certain he's getting everything he needs!''

''Shh,'' he said, pulling her close to him so that she was enveloped against his chest. ''I have the main hospital being searched. That's where he'll be found.''

''How do you know?'' she asked, her voice watery.

''Because for every harebrained angle I come up with, I come up with one that's dead-on. Every time.''

She stared up at him, her shamrock-green eyes hopeful. ''You really think he's that close? I'll go search every room myself.''

He had to smile at her earnestness. There was nothing this lady wouldn't do for the children in her care. ''You stay here with the babies, and I'll do the searching. Okay?'' he asked, gently stroking her hair back from her face. ''Isn't that the way it's always been between the sexes? Woman nurtures, man hunts and protects.''

Her shoulders went stiff as she jerked out of his arms, just as he'd known she would. A devilish smile leaped onto his face. ''That's the lady I know, the one with the iron spine and the spirit of the Tartars.''

''The what?'' she demanded.

''Never mind. I've got a baby to locate. Although I'm expecting Matthew to return in his runaway isolette any moment now. Remember that in cases of

newborns kidnapped from hospitals, they are almost
always found quickly. Someone will notice when a
new baby turns up unexpectedly somewhere." And
then, because she looked so put out with him, he
reached out and touched the side of her lips, gently
turning one corner of her mouth up. "Later on, I
want you to smile for me, April."

"Why?"

He laughed at her pugnacious question. "Because
you make me feel warm when you smile that big
smile of yours."

The wheels were turning in her head; he could
nearly hear them whirring at full speed. She was
trying to figure out exactly what he wanted from her,
besides the smile.

But there was nothing he wanted.

Except, maybe, quite possibly, her.

He shut the voice out of his mind, told himself it
would never work, and left to do a little detective
work, something that never failed to put his mind
on a single track.

This time it didn't work.

When this child is found, he vowed, *I'm going to
offer April the only thing I have to give her: my
protection. All these children can be under one roof,
safe. In April's arms, safe. And together, safe.*

IT WASN'T THAT HARD to locate the baby. Caleb
merely had to put himself in the shoes of a desperate
person, likely female, likely recently disappointed in

a birth process, and he headed to the main birth wing at Maitland Maternity.

A quick count at the nursery window showed ten newborns engaged in healthy squalling or being fed by attentive nurses. "I'm Caleb McCallum from the McCallum wing. Are these all the viable deliveries within the last twenty-four hours?" he asked a nurse.

"These are all of them. We only had one unsuccessful delivery—the placenta separated and caused problems."

"Where is the mother?"

"In her room, resting."

"Are you certain?"

The nurse's eyebrow shot up. "Come with me, Mr. McCallum."

Indeed, the mother was resting. Sitting up, she slept, at peace with the world, no doubt dreaming of happy moments she had waited for nine months to experience. One of her hands was in the plastic bassinet pulled up next to her bed, resting gently upon a sleeping baby's back.

Matthew.

"That baby shouldn't be in here," the nurse gasped.

Caleb put his hand on the nurse's arm. "It's all right," he said softly. "She hasn't done any real harm. If I were you, I'd talk to the head nurse about getting a grief counselor to this woman immediately."

"But the baby—"

"I'll take him back. He belongs in the McCallum wing."

"If you're certain—"

She clearly was not, as the whole situation was terribly out of order. But Caleb was more concerned about the grieving birth mother. "Let's put our focus on the mother. This baby has a lot of people cheering for him, but she..." His voice faltered as he looked back at the mother. All she'd wanted was to feel the precious skin of a child. Sometimes a simple touch could mean everything in a moment of despondency. "I'll get the baby."

As soon as he touched Matthew's bassinet, the mother's eyes snapped open. "It's okay," he said, putting his hand over hers. "I'm just going to take Matthew back to the nursery now. He needs special care." He massaged her fingers gently in his before moving her hand from the baby's back. "Thank you for watching over him."

"I just wanted to—"

"Shh. I know. Go back to sleep," he told her, his tone soothing. "You need special care and rest now, too."

"I didn't mean any harm, I just—"

"It's okay," he repeated reassuringly. "You're not in any trouble, but we do have to take Matthew back where he belongs. Right now, you need to rest." He smiled at her, focusing calm on her so that she would relax.

"Thank you," she whispered as she closed her eyes, exhausted.

"Go to sleep," he softly commanded, stealthily wheeling Matthew from the room.

The nurse followed in astonishment. "You handled that like a police officer talking a jumper off a bridge."

"Thanks," Caleb said grimly. "I'm taking Matthew back to McCallum." He rolled the isolette in front of him, his heart thundering as he stared at the tiny bundle of life, innocently unaware that his disappearance had caused an uproar. "Little man, back you go in your flying isolette. I know several people who are going to be delighted to see you, and one spicy little nurse in particular."

CALEB WASN'T CERTAIN where the idea came from. It hit in the split second after he wheeled Matthew beside the nursery window. The squeal of pure joy that left April's throat as she flew into the hall seared his brain with the fear she'd suffered, and he'd instantly thought, *I can do something about that.*

"April," he said as she prepared to wheel the bassinet into the nursery, "I think we ought to get married."

Chapter Five

In her overwhelming relief at having Matthew back, April wasn't certain she'd heard Caleb right when he spoke. Or maybe he was teasing. Concern was flying through her mind as her eager fingers touched Matthew's skin, checking him over as the nurse and the mother in her warred to know he was safe and sound; perhaps she'd missed the resonance in Caleb's flat comment. Men didn't deliver proposals the way he had, did they? And why would he want to marry her?

"I'm sorry, Caleb, I wasn't listening. Could you repeat that?"

A muscle twitched in his jaw; his Adam's apple jumped in his throat. "Maybe we ought to get married."

She searched his face for signs of teasing, reluctance, medication, *anything*. But his expression was genuine, his posture stiff.

He was *serious*.

"Let me put Matthew back into the nursery. I

want to change him, and get him where he can hear his brother and sisters. And then we'll talk. Okay?''

He nodded, and April wheeled the bassinet into the nursery, her heart thundering. *My first proposal. And I don't think it's because he's in love with me, either.*

Her hands shook as she fixed Matthew's diaper, and then checked the other babies. Making a notation on the charts, she counted to ten, tried to gather her courage and went out into the hall to meet Caleb.

''Where was he?'' she asked, unable to help herself.

''At Maitland. A mother had an unsuccessful pregnancy and was distraught. I'm guessing she crept down here during the early shift, when the desk wasn't fully staffed. She just wanted to touch a living, breathing baby, I believe, in order to save herself from—'' he blew out a breath ''—I don't know. Probably going around the bend.''

''Oh, poor thing,'' April said, her heart struck. ''I wouldn't want to be in her shoes. I mean, she shouldn't have done it, and technically, the hospital should—''

''Let's not go into technicalities right now. I asked you a question, April,'' he said.

She swallowed uncertainly, perceiving that he might have blurted out the question, surprising even himself, but she knew there was some strong reasoning behind it.

''Not that this is the first thing I thought I'd say

when I received my first proposal, but why?'' she asked him.

''You're not going to get temporary custody without a two-parent home. I'm willing to provide that.''

''Why?'' she asked again, unable to see where he was heading.

''Because I can. And I don't want them shuffled off, either. And it scared the hell out of me when Matthew was missing. If I have all five of you under one roof, I can...you know.''

April cocked her head. ''Protect us better?'' she asked softly.

''Of course.''

She sensed behind his brisk tone that he was hiding his feelings as much as she was. ''I don't know what to say.''

''It makes sense.''

''Yes, in a strange sort of way. We'd have to file for emergency temporary custody. It's possible. But...that's an awful lot of adjustment for you, Caleb. Four babies, a wife, a very small house, diapers, crying, feeding—''

''I hope you don't cry too much,'' Caleb said. ''As for feeding, there's always fast food. Cops are used to eating on the run.''

''I meant the babies.''

Caleb gave her an abashed grin. ''I knew what you meant. I'm trying to inject some levity into a moment where my heart's about to leap out of my chest. I don't do much of anything without a lot of methodical thought, so I've just about used up my allotment of proposal courage.''

"Oh, that's sweet of you, Caleb," April said quietly. "Here comes your father."

To her astonishment, Caleb turned pale before her very eyes. *He really hasn't thought this through,* she realized.

And in a way, she liked the fact that he hadn't calculated what his proposal would mean in terms of turning his life upside down and inside out.

"Mr. McCallum, my best friend, your daughter, Bri, is not the only McCallum to marry, it seems. Your son has just asked me to marry him," April said to Jackson as he joined them in the viewing area.

"He has?" Jackson seemed stunned as his gaze riveted to their faces.

"Yes. I'd like to know what you think about that."

The elderly man eyed his son with some amazement. "That you're getting the short end of the stick, April, but if you think you can put up with him…" His attempt at teasing fell flat as his hope caught up inside him. He stared at Caleb. "I didn't know you were contemplating such a serious move."

Caleb shrugged. "I didn't, either. But the time feels right."

Jackson scratched his head, glancing at April.

"Um, how can I put this delicately? Is there—or will there be—a grandchild in the mix?"

Apparently, Jackson thought that there had been some nights of passion between April and Caleb, a quick fling even, and there were results for which to be accounted. April smiled at him, and then glanced toward the four babies in their isolettes. "We hope so. That's the main idea."

Jackson followed her gaze, then snapped his own to his son's face. Caleb stared back at him, unperturbed. Slowly, Jackson glanced at the babies, then brought his focus to the hint of a smile on April's face. "Oh, I see," he said softly. "I do see. Well, thank you for letting me in on the scheme. I'll do everything I can to help you."

He kissed April on both cheeks, his style old world, and April sensed he was being chivalrous in a moment that had totally knocked him off his feet. Clearing his throat, he said gruffly, "April, what I said about you getting the short end of the stick—" he glanced toward Caleb "—I'm very proud of my son. I don't always show it."

Her smile was understanding. "I know, Mr. McCallum."

"Jackson. You're going to be part of the family." He shook his son's hand, took April's hand in his, and as he stood in between them, keeping a tight hold on both, he looked through the nursery window. "Quadruplets," he said under his breath. "I'd better get busy!"

"Well, we don't have our hopes up too high," April said. "And rest assured that we will have a prenuptial agreement drawn up."

"Prenuptial agreement?" Caleb and Jackson echoed.

"Of course. In the event that…our situation doesn't come to fruition, I wouldn't want you to think that you have any lingering responsibilities for me. Or to me."

"A prenup is not necessary, April." Caleb looked stoney.

"I feel it is," she said, her tone quiet yet firm. "It's very important to me that all the expectations are known by everyone up front. I'm doing this for the children, not for me, or for you. You're giving me your name, and a marriage contract for a clearcut reason, and I feel that I should treat it as such."

"Well, I don't think—" Caleb began.

"I think April has hit upon a very sensible arrangement, myself. After all, there are all my millions at stake, and a prenup would make me rest easier at night."

April smiled. "Precisely what I was thinking."

"Now, wait just a minute—" Caleb tried again.

"Caleb, can I see you in private?" Jackson asked. "Congratulations, April, I think this is a very satisfactory arrangement for everyone. I am delighted to welcome such a forward-thinking and intelligent woman into our family, for however long."

"Thank you, Jackson."

"If you'll excuse us..." Caleb said reluctantly.

"Of course." April smiled at him, and walked back into the nursery, touching each child with fingers that gently, firmly pressed their skin. So that they would know she was there. And that she loved them.

JACKSON FAIRLY DRAGGED his son into the Austin Eats diner next to the hospital. "I don't have to tell you how happy I am about this, son."

Caleb sank into a booth. "I'm not certain what I am."

"Look. Let the prenup thing go. The girl is obviously independent, and wants us to know she doesn't expect anything from us."

"From me, Dad, she's marrying *me*."

"Not exactly. When you marry someone, you marry the in-laws too, Caleb. And that means *me*— and my money, about which she's trying to reassure me. I say give April her breathing room. Who cares about the prenup?"

"I do. I don't think a marriage starts well with a road map. You and Mom didn't have one."

"Well, your mother was a delicate little flower who did everything I wanted and lived to please me. I haven't married again because I'll never find that kind of devotion."

"April's a delicate flower—"

"Not really, son. She got that spine of independence from somewhere. I say, tell her our lawyer will draw up the prenup, and then, I suspect you two will be so busy that she'll forget that the lawyer doesn't get around to it.''

Caleb frowned. ''Are you saying we'll trick her?''

''No, I'm saying that I don't think we really need to go to the trouble with this gal. If you don't get the children, and you decide not to stay together, you'll just annul the marriage. Right?''

He didn't want to think about that scenario—it meant admitting that April might not get temporary custody of the children, and it meant she might not want to stay with him if she didn't. He really didn't like that thought.

''I don't think I like it, Dad.''

''Look.'' Jackson blew out a breath and scratched his white-maned head. ''Ever since your mom was gone, you've wanted reassurance from everyone that they weren't going to leave you. You didn't realize it, but that's what you were doing. When your partner died, you took it hard, which is natural, especially since you blamed yourself. But you never got over it because it was a piece of yourself you couldn't hang on to. That's left over from your mom's death. I've stayed a little aloof from you over the years because I was worried about how you'd take it if I up and croaked. You took your mother's death harder than the other kids, Caleb.''

''There was a reason for that,'' Caleb said on a growl.

''I know. I know. Self-induced guilt,'' Jackson

said. "But it's time you let go, son, and realize that you can't hold on to people so tight. You're gonna scare this little girl, because all she wants is to think she's always gonna have her independence. You see how this is a recipe for sure disaster?"

A glimmer of recognition was starting to intrude in his brain, and Caleb didn't want to let it in. "Not really."

"Okay." Jackson put the saltshaker in the middle of the table. "This is April. She's salty and independent because she's had to be that way. This is you," he said, placing the pepper shaker next to April the saltshaker. "You want to share the same space with her, but you can't. You can't go on watermelon, you can't go in ice cream, you can't go in cookies."

"You are making no sense at all."

"You can't make the pepper go where the salt wants to every time, or you'll ruin the recipe," Jackson said, out of patience. "Isn't there a rock song that has to do with if you love something, you gotta let it go? She wants her independence; you can't hold on to her so tightly. Pretend the prenup is okay with you, and she'll appreciate you for it, Caleb. It's the first thing you can do that shows April you're not going to try to squash her with overbearing solicitousness."

Caleb shook his head at his father. "I want to take care of her. That's my end of the bargain."

"And she doesn't want you to," Jackson said

stubbornly. "You can't hold on to everything with both fists, son. Life is fleeting, like water in your hands."

"All right," Caleb finally said on a sigh. "I'll try not to squish her."

"Squash."

"Whatever. Oh, Jeez, I can't believe this."

"Well, I never got around to the birds-and-the-bees talk with you when you were a teen, so now I figure having a chat that keeps you from putting your big foot on top of your newly budding engagement makes up for it."

The waitress came to their table. Jackson ordered chicken and mushroom chowder, and Caleb ordered a cheeseburger—not that he really had any appetite.

"You know, Caleb, it's probably time for you to let that bag of guilt go, especially before you get married."

"What bag of guilt?" Caleb demanded, certain he didn't want to have this conversation.

"About your mom." Jackson looked out the window at the hospital for a moment, then brought his gaze back to his son. "There isn't a week that goes by that I don't think maybe it was my fault. I knew she was a fragile little thing. But, Caleb, babies were what your mom wanted. It's what made her happy. Her health never entered her mind, not by the doctor's caution or my worrying."

He stared at his son. "Think about that. I had the chance to say, 'Have a selective elimination procedure.' But I didn't, because three was what God had given her, and that's what she wanted. Yet, also a single day never went by in our children's childhoods where I didn't think why her? Why not me? She was the one who wanted these babies, she carried them, she worked for them, she endured the pain to carry and deliver them. And then she never got to enjoy the blessings she so dreamed of.''

Caleb thought about the suffering woman in the hospital who had felt the same way. It was almost as if, for one split second he'd seen his mother in her. Tears pricked the corners of his eyes. Impatiently, he rubbed at them, demanding that they retreat.

''Great gravy, son, if anyone should have been feeling guilty, it was me. But no little innocent baby had anything to do with her death.''

Caleb sighed as the waitress put their food in front of them. ''April is very delicate, too.''

''Yes, and you can't do a damn thing about that. If you love her, then accept that she has to make some choices for herself, and you gotta let her.''

He stared into his father's compassionate gaze. ''All right,'' he said finally. ''I'll bow to your wisdom and experience on this one.''

Jackson nodded slowly, his gaze appreciative and empathetic, too, and for the first time in his life, Caleb felt a bond growing between them.

''So, how long is this supposed to last?'' Jackson asked.

"We discussed filing for emergency temporary custody until the birth mother returns. April really believes that since Jenny left them to her, it's up to her to keep the babies from being parceled out among strangers."

"I couldn't agree more." He was thoughtful for a moment. "You know, son, if you go slowly, bit by bit, this marriage agreement might stick longer than April plans for it to."

"I don't think I should expect more from it than I know it to be, Dad."

Jackson waved that away. "I didn't say anything about expecting. I said, if you go slowly and gently, treading lightly, she just might learn to trust you. And then to love you."

"You make it sound so easy."

His father shrugged. "If anyone can put themselves in April's place, I'd put my money on you. Bit by bit, son. No leaping tall buildings in a single bound. Just a nice, slow walk holding each other's hand can conquer a path of great resistance."

Jackson took a spoonful of soup, and then as an afterthought, stared at his son. "She *did* say yes, didn't she? Or did she just give us a bunch of qualifications?"

APRIL'S HEART was still fluttering over Caleb's surprise proposal when she left work. She hadn't even mentioned it to Cherilyn or Bri, she was that rattled.

When she saw Caleb walking toward her in the

parking lot, bearing florist-wrapped long-stemmed roses, her heart went into full-speed motion sickness. "You really mean it," she said when he came abreast of her.

"Of course. No man fools around with the M-word unless he means it."

"Oh…" Shyly, she buried her nose among the red, satiny blooms of the roses. "They're lovely. Thank you."

"I was afraid maybe I didn't hear you accept me," Caleb said, his face serious. "If you hadn't yet, I thought I'd better do a little better in the convincing department." And he pulled out a jeweler's box, handing it to her opened, so she could see the lovely emerald-shaped diamond inside. "Four sides to this stone, four babies in our lives. I hope you'll say yes, April."

She nearly dropped the roses. Heck, she thought she was going to faint. "Caleb! You don't have to give me a ring! It's just something I have to give back once Jenny returns."

"No." He shook his head, staring into her eyes. "It's for you, April. You gave me a gift I've wanted all my life, the beginning of a relationship with my father. We're actually relating to each other rather than not relating at all. This is yours, no strings attached. No prenup needed for this." And taking the ring from the box, he slipped it onto her finger. "Besides, we want everyone to believe that we're in love, and ready to be a happy family of six."

"Oh, Caleb." Surprised tears jumped into her eyes. "I have said yes, haven't I? Because if I haven't, *yes*. And thank you so much for taking up my cause. You're the knight I hadn't expected, and you can't possibly know how much it means to me."

They looked at each other for a few moments, awkwardly. April wondered if he was going to kiss her, or if she should just reach up and kiss him.

In the end, that's what she did.

And when he wrapped his arms around her, heedless of the roses, April realized this big, strong man had given her a gift she'd wanted all her life, too.

Babies of her very own.

Even if it was only temporary.

Chapter Six

"I suppose I shouldn't have done that," April said, pulling away, immediately aware of strange longings rushing through her, longings that had nothing to do with wanting to stop at a friendly kiss. The moment their lips touched and he wrapped his arms around her to enclose her against his chest, her brain had instantly responded *Oh, yes, oh my stars, yes*.

What her mind and body were saying yes to was so much different than what she'd expected to want from Caleb. It was best if she remembered that this was pretend. Their relationship had a goal: the well-being of four children.

"It was fine by me," Caleb said, his hands in his jeans pockets, looking incredibly handsome for a man she didn't want to recognize in this sexy manner. His gaze was level, open and intense. Very aware of her as a woman.

Shivers claimed her skin; her nipples tightened, and the most feminine area of her body went warm with desire.

I'm in way over my head with this man.

She calmed herself with rationale. There really wasn't any rhyme or reason for her to get side-tracked by Caleb's enormous capacity for making her feel like a treasured doll. She knew all about collecting and caretaking of wonderful things. Yet she also knew from painful experience that her heartstrings snapped long before any man managed to get her down the aisle in a real wedding. The only way she'd manage to get through this wedding was because it was fake. A faux fiancé. She couldn't bend enough to allow a man to take care of her, as if she were a collectible doll. Being forced to learn to rely solely upon herself was a blessing in many ways; yet it had also left her with the inability to structure a lasting relationship.

This one wouldn't be any different—unless it remained a masquerade for Social Services.

So why had her heart jumped like a heartbeat on a monitor when he'd kissed her? She'd nearly melted into a feminine puddle of desire—and she had a funny feeling he was completely aware that he'd had her guard down for a split second.

Like the time she'd caught him staring at her posterior. It was a crack in his armor, and she'd kind of liked seeing him check her out.

By the fiery burn in his gaze, she was pretty certain he was enjoying this crack in *her* armor.

"I have to go," she murmured swiftly, holding

the roses in front of her like a shield. "Thank you, Caleb. For everything."

She made her escape as quickly as she could, totally aware that she was running like a scared rabbit that flees, uncertain as to what it's fleeing from, but the scent of danger hurrying it ever faster.

April couldn't get to the shelter of her home fast enough.

THERE WERE A FEW THINGS Caleb knew for certain after April's impulsive kiss. She'd been touched by the ring, if only for the sake of the ruse they were perpetrating. She wasn't immune to him. Her lips felt like a dream under his, soft and supple and clinging, the way he liked a woman's lips to be.

And she was scared to death of liking him. This marriage was all about the babies, and there was no subtle trap waiting to spring its jaws on him. She wasn't marrying him with the notion that she needed a husband, or that the situation was a good way to rope him blindly into something long-term.

Oh, no. She'd innocently kissed him, and been very startled by the blaze that had very nearly erupted. He'd felt her tremble in his arms.

That tremble had told him everything a man needed to know about a woman. She was attracted to him—and she was going to fight her feelings every step of the way.

He'd just have to help her make up her mind to

allow him to kiss her again and this time not cut it so dramatically short. *The next time I kiss her, she won't go running from my arms. She'll stay—because she wants to.*

Chapter Seven

There wasn't a moment to waste. As soon as the mandatory blood tests had been reviewed and the marriage license waiting period ended, Caleb McCallum married April Sullivan in a quiet court-house ceremony performed in a justice of the peace's chambers.

All the while, April's heart was in her throat. Caleb held her hand despite the delicate bouquet of white roses she clutched. She could feel a tiny pulse in his thumb.

The moment felt all too real to her for something that was supposed to be simulated. She was certain her skin could not have felt more moist, her pulse more erratic, if this was a wedding for keeps.

Jackson looked so proud of his son. Though it was a daytime ceremony during courthouse hours— noon, before the courthouse closed for New Year's—he wore an elegantly formal charcoal-gray suit, with a black-and-white striped tie so satiny it could have complemented a tux. Caleb wore a suit strikingly similar, which made his short dark hair and hazel eyes stand out richly.

He's so incredibly handsome, April thought. *And so giving.*

Between Caleb and Jackson, she felt as if she would be well protected. It was clear they were determined to take care of her, a thought that both comforted and worried her.

Bri looked fetching in a short pink dress, suitable for tonight's New Year's Eve dinner at the McCallum mansion. Jackson had insisted the whole family get together for dinner to celebrate both the wedding and the new year. *A wedding and a new year—we'll ring them in together,* he'd said.

April felt a tiny chip of reluctance drop from her heart as Adam gave Caleb a brotherly pound of congratulations on the shoulder when the ceremony ended.

And then Bri kissed her cheek, murmuring, "I never thought I'd see this day, and I couldn't be any happier, even if that was the shortest dating period in history. One night. Wow."

April embraced her new sister-in-law, remembering all the times she had thought Bri was the closest thing to a sister she'd ever have. And now she was—for a while.

Caleb, Jackson and April had agreed not to tell anyone that the marriage was short-term, a means to an end, in case Social Services might get wind of the posthaste wedding and decide to question the circumstances.

"Thank you, Bri," April said, hugging her tightly as she told the tears at the corners of her eyes to stay in place.

"You've made my father so happy," Bri said. "He thought Caleb would turn to stone before he allowed anyone to get close to him."

April separated herself from her best friend and now sister. Caleb put his arm around her. "Mrs. McCallum," he said, his voice unsteady, "you look wonderful."

She felt a blush tint her cheeks as she looked up at him. Not for anything would she admit that when she'd tried on this short wedding dress in a vintage clothing store, she'd been struck by its simplicity and charm. It had a short fingertip veil as well, but she'd left that at home, content to make do with the fifties-style wedding gown. The style wasn't incongruous in a courthouse, yet she felt very fairy-tale princess. The dress had been a bit pricey for her budget, but she'd bought it anyway, something in her heart wanting very much for Caleb not to be disappointed in his bride.

"I'm glad you think so," she said nervously, wondering if she could be any more unsettled if this moment were the real thing. "You're very handsome, too."

Caleb winked at her. "Did you expect anything else?"

Bri popped him lightly on the shoulder. "Behave, or April might change her mind."

"She can't. She's mine, fair and square."

Ringing began in April's ears, running through her brain. Her hands began to tremble, and her stomach pitched. "I think I'll get a drink of water," she said breathlessly, heading toward the courtroom exit.

The rows of the courthouse were full of strangers, but April paid them no attention as she hurried past. She had to get out of there fast, before she began to get lost somewhere between the reason and the reality of her new situation.

"Slow down, April," Caleb said, catching up to her and taking her hand in his.

They were outside the main courtroom now, and she could take in more than a stifled breath of air.

"Was it getting to you?" Caleb asked.

"A little," April admitted. "I didn't expect it to feel so real! All your family, I mean, I didn't even think to ask my mom and dad because this is just pretend. I wasn't even planning to tell them, and now I feel horrible, like I've left them out of something really important."

"Focus, April," he whispered against her hair. "Day after tomorrow, we file an emergency application with Social Services. That starts the interviewing process, I'm certain. Meanwhile, I'll be hunting Jenny for all I'm worth. You'll be back at work keeping an eye on the little muffins, and all will be good."

An unbridelike sniffle escaped her. "You're right, of course."

"Of course I am." Patting her back as he held her close to him, he said, "Pull yourself together and act like a happy bride or Bri is going to yell at me. All right?" he asked gently, wiping the tears from the sides of her eyes.

"You're an annoyingly confident male, do you know that?" she asked, pushing his hands away so she could wipe her own face, but smiling at him just the same.

"I expect to hear you say that many times in the course of our short marriage. And if you're worried about your folks, why don't you and I go by and get them and have them to Dad's house for dinner?"

"Would he mind?" April asked.

"He'd be delighted. He asked me if your parents were coming today, and I told him we hadn't discussed it. I didn't know how you'd want to handle it."

"Well, I just can't all of a sudden be up and living with you, I guess," April said. "They'd wonder when I'd met you."

"They're going to wonder anyway, since we're married. We'll have to tell them we eloped to save on money."

April laughed. "You think of everything, don't you?"

"Every angle, lady, and any angle can be promising. Now come back with me before Jackson thinks I've got a runaway bride on my hands.''

She smiled, feeling better now that her head had cleared. "I'm better now.''

"I hope so," Caleb said, taking her hand in his. "Because if you freaked out thinking the wedding was real, us living under the same roof may be shaky.''

"As little shaking as possible," she reminded him.

"That's right. I just wanted to see if you remembered.''

She remembered, all right. It almost dimmed the beauty of the marital vows they'd just spoken.

THE ENORMITY OF WHAT he and April had done came rolling in on Caleb as they drove up in the driveway of the Sullivans' small home. He'd married her—and never given a thought to asking her father for her hand.

Of course, that's because their marriage agreement had been fast, and tied to four young babies. But if he'd been marrying her for real, he would have asked her father's permission first.

Walking in to a stranger's house and announcing he was now family was going to be fairly wild for a man who didn't like change.

"Why am I suddenly feeling apprehensive?" he asked out loud.

"Same reason I felt apprehensive after your family began congratulating me?'' April guessed. ''It feels like we're lying.''

''We *are* posturing, but in the most honorable sense.''

''I guess there's such a thing. I'm telling myself this is okay. But I think my parents are going to be so...well, so surprised.''

''Unpleasantly so.''

''Maybe. They couldn't have children, and so they adopted me, and they've kind of lived vicariously through me. And they're older, quite a bit older than your father.''

''Well,'' he said, sighing, ''we'll sound cracked if we tell them we did this in the hopes that we can foster four children until I can find the birth mother.''

April bit her lip. He wanted to lay a finger against her soft skin to stop her, but if he did, he'd probably start kissing her, and then they'd never get inside the house. ''I didn't kiss you after we got married,'' he said suddenly.

''No, you didn't. I assumed it was because we were in the justice's chambers.''

Caleb shook his head. ''No, I think I was worried about you because I could feel you trembling.''

''I could feel the pulse in your thumb,'' she said, giving him a cautious look. ''I think you were nervous.''

''If you felt my thumb right now, you'd *know* I'm nervous.'' An elderly gentleman came out onto the

porch to stare at their car. Caleb took a deep breath
as the man waved to them, and without further hesitation, he got out of the Acura.

"You coming in or not?" April's adoptive father
shouted.

Hard-of-hearing, Caleb guessed. "Yes, sir," he
called back loudly. "Let me get April."

Opening April's car door, he helped her out. "Did
I tell you you're stunningly beautiful?" he whispered urgently.

"No, you didn't, but thanks." She hurried up the
slate steps to kiss her father. "Hi, Daddy."

"April, love. You should have let us know you
were bringing a gentleman by. We would have had
some supper for him."

Her mother came out on the porch as well, looking with pride at April's beautiful dress. "My, don't
you look lovely, April. And your gentleman friend
is so handsome."

"Thanks, Mom, Dad." April glanced at Caleb,
and he shrugged at her. The twitch in his thumb had
moved to his eye, and he was pretty certain that, if
they didn't get on with the big announcement and
whatever reaction was due him, he was going to
have a tic for life.

"Well, bring him in," her mother told her.
"Please do come in, Mr.—"

"Mom, this is Caleb McCallum," April said
quickly. "Caleb, this is my mother, Donna, and my
father, Webb."

"Well, bring him in, April. We don't want him to think we're rude the first time your friend meets us."

Caleb held the door open for the two fragile people. April lingered to whisper, "This is not going to be easy."

"I wasn't signed on for easy, remember. I'm okay with it," he said, not one hundred percent truthful but telling himself a brave front could make up for the percentage he was fibbing. "When this is all over, I'll let you kiss me."

April ignored that.

Donna perched on a green velvet antique sofa, and Webb gestured to a rocking chair for Caleb. That left no place for April and him to sit together, which might have been her father's intention. He wasn't certain. April went to sit by her mother, who clasped her hand.

"You see, Mom, Dad," she said, swallowing. Caleb could tell she was nervous. "Caleb and I got married today."

Both the Sullivans stared at Caleb.

The room went deathly quiet.

"Why?" Donna asked.

Caleb stared at their hopeful faces, realizing that they wanted a reassuring explanation. Hopes and dreams lay in their curious eyes as both parents waited patiently. April was the child they'd adopted late in her childhood, late in their life. They wanted to know that he loved their only child.

He thought about the way he'd wanted to find Bri's boyfriend and make him marry his sister when he'd learned she was pregnant.

Caleb wanted to know that Bri would be loved. Bri wouldn't tell anyone the name of the father of her babies. Hunter Callaghan had come to the wing to become its administrator and reunited with Bri. He thought about the immature writing of Jenny's note, as she left her children to the one person she knew would love them.

What the Sullivans wanted badly to hear was so understandable, so normal, that it had him sweating in his suit. His shirt collar felt stiff as he swallowed.

"Because I love her," he said.

April GASPED at Caleb's unexpected pronouncement. Her mother clasped her hands together with delight. "Oh, I couldn't be happier," she said with sparkly tears in her eyes. "I can't tell you how we've waited, hoping that a young gentleman would see all the gifts April has to offer a man. Webb and I were so afraid we'd pass on before the right man discovered our special girl." Donna got up to cross to the rocker, taking Caleb's hands in hers. "Welcome to the family," she said to Caleb, kissing his cheek.

Webb gruffly cleared his throat. "Yes. Welcome to the family."

"Wait. I've got something for you, April." Donna rushed from the room, returning a second later with a cameo. "It was my mother's on her wedding day, and mine when I married Webb, and now it's yours." Gently, she clasped the antique necklace around April's neck. "And doesn't that go just beautifully with her hair?" she proudly asked Caleb.

April flushed, still overcome by his declaration. He didn't mean it, did he? Love was not in their agreement. Of course he didn't love her. He was merely trying to make her elderly parents happy.

"Just think, Webb," Donna said happily. "We could even be grandparents before we pass on. Wouldn't that be a miracle?"

April leaned back against the high-backed sofa as she caught Caleb's eye. She was expecting a wink of job-well-done or something of the sort, but his expression was so solemn that it made her uncomfortable.

"And you love him, too, April?" Webb asked. "This marriage is what you wanted?"

How could she lie to her parents? They both stared at her so hopefully, waiting for her to say that this was the man she had waited for all her life, this was the man who made her dreams come true. After all their love and care in raising her, she'd found the man who could give her what they wanted her to have.

Caleb watched her, and if she didn't know better, she'd think he was holding his breath. His tie looked tight on his neck.

"Yes," she said, her whole being miserable.

Chapter Eight

"You said it first," April told Caleb in the car after they'd left her parents' house. Donna and Webb weren't used to getting out much, and the cold weather seemed an invitation to light rain and slick streets, so they'd declined to come to the party at Jackson's house. "You said it, which made *me* have to say it."

Caleb snorted. "I haven't had much practice with in-laws. I couldn't let them down."

"I couldn't, either," April said. She stared out the window at the streets that seemed hard with the freeze.

"I thought they took our marriage well." He glanced at her, noting that her face was strained. "And we get to fake it for my family tonight, and the hospital staff tomorrow, and after that, Social Services. Piece of cake."

"My parents will be so disappointed when we divorce."

He scratched the back of his neck as he braked at

a stop sign. April's low voice told him she was wondering if she'd made a mistake. And maybe they had. "Are you regretting our marriage?"

"I don't think so." She sighed, stretching her arms around her knees. "I'm not regretting it at all for the babies, if we can keep them together. I do feel a little sorry for my folks. They had their own dreams for me."

The intersection was clear of cars, so he moved the Acura forward. He didn't suffer April's worries, because his father was in on the "scheme," as Jackson had called it. Clear as anything, Caleb had read the Sullivans' hopes, too. They wanted the prince to come riding up for their daughter, and reassure them that in their old age, they had nothing to worry about where she was concerned. She'd be loved, and taken care of, and swept off to his castle.

He didn't have a castle. And he wasn't much of a prince.

"Do you want to talk about living arrangements?" he asked, trying to get her mind off her parents. "Now that we're getting the big stuff out of the way, maybe we ought to talk about the incidentals, such as keeping up a good front."

"You could…move into my house."

The dollhouse? "Do you think that's a good idea?" he asked carefully.

"Well, we can't raise four babies in an apartment. I mean, we can, but there's no reason, since I have a house. And a yard for them to play in."

He frowned. "I don't know if I can live in your house."

"I don't know if you can, either," April said. "You're going to have to get a futon or a rollaway."

"A futon?" he yelped.

"You won't fit into my bed, unless you're lying right on top of me."

"Well, now, there's an idea."

"No. There is not an idea." April shook her head to discourage such notions, even though she knew he'd been teasing her—to a point. But it was a point she didn't even want to bring into the conversation. "We said nothing about marital relations when we discussed the prenup."

"Wait a minute. The prenup was about money, wasn't it?"

"That, among other things. The prenup is about independence, you see."

Caleb pulled up in front of the McCallum mansion, parked the car, turned off the engine and turned to look at her. "I do not see."

"I keep my house, you keep your apartment. You keep your car, I keep mine. You get a futon, I sleep alone. Independence."

He blinked. "Forever?"

"Caleb, you're not really my husband."

She looked confused but beautiful in her innocence—white gown and pretty, upswept hair. Caleb wasn't sure how long he could live with her without being driven mad. "Maybe I should stay in my own apartment."

"You could," April said brightly. "At least until we find out if we get the babies."

"You don't want me with you at your house, do you?"

Her eyes softened as she looked at him. "I'm not sure I do."

"I promise to put the lid down on the toilet and the cap back on the toothpaste."

"Why do you *want* to stay in my house?"

He couldn't say for sure; he was only teasing her right now because he could tell she was resisting him so badly. "You're worried that I'm going to try to claim my husbandly rights."

"Oh, for heaven's sakes!" She crossed her arms and stared forward through the windshield. "I kissed *you,* if you recall, not the other way around."

"So you did." He wound the slight tendril that had escaped her hairdo around his finger. "And I liked it."

Her lips twitched with reluctance. "I didn't."

Gently, he tugged the tendril. "That is the second fib you've told today."

"It's the third. I said I'd love you and cherish you and keep you, or something to that effect. And we know that's not going to happen."

"Well, you're turning into a real dishonest young bride." He tsk-tsked her. "Maybe you're being dishonest about the reason you don't want me to stay in your house.''

''There really isn't any reason for it, is there? You probably watch wrestling. I'd go mad.''

''You'd probably want me to mow the yard and learn how to make string pot holders. *I'd* go mad.''

That made her laugh, and he moved his finger from her hair to the back of her bare neck, stroking lightly. ''It's happened fast, but it doesn't have to be fast between us, April.''

She turned to look at him. ''Do you mean it?''

''Of course. I know what my role in this charade is.''

''It's not a charade. You're kind to try to help me.''

''I like it when you're grateful,'' he teased. ''It makes me want to kiss you.''

''Caleb!'' She flicked his hand from her neck, but her tone wasn't angry.

''I think I know what you're worried about,'' he said quietly. ''And I'm not going to expect you to become 'my woman,''' he said, the final words in a gruff, manly tone.

''Your woman?''

''Yeah. Kind of like the caveman days. I promise not to drag you off by the hair and—that's why you won't come to my apartment, isn't it? You're afraid to leave your safe little nest to come to my cave.''

A charming moment of hesitation gave her away. *''No,''* she denied vehemently.

"Yes you are! April Sullivan-McCallum," he said, sticking a hand under her ribs to tickle her, "your nose is growing a foot. You're afraid I'm going to sweep you off your feet, carry you off to my cave and ravish you."

Her pert nose went into the air as she caught his hand in hers, stilling him. "I cannot be swept, carried or ravished."

His eyebrow lifted. "Why not?"

"I won't allow it." And she opened the car door, hurrying to the mansion door, her white puffy skirt billowing in the cold New Year's Eve breeze.

"Is this a battle-of-the-sexes kind of thing?" he called after her, slamming the door as he followed. "Mrs. McCallum, I promise never to encroach upon your emotional territory. That's a vow I can keep."

She waited for him on the long porch. "You told my parents you loved me. That made *me* have to say it."

"Yes, but it made them so happy." Taking her face between his palms, he captured her lips in a surprise kiss.

"Oh," Bri exclaimed as she suddenly opened the door. "You *do* love her, don't you, Caleb? I did wonder, but then I could tell you did in the courthouse. It was written all over your face!"

Now he was trapped, fair and square. Bri's expression was so delighted. He couldn't bear to disappoint her. April stared up at him, her emerald eyes huge, and he could feel her holding her breath.

Well, this whole conversation was about independence. Little Miss Freedom was determined to keep him at bay, with a prenup and any other thing she could think of.

But he was holding her now and that's what made this New Year's Eve moment so special. He had her face in his hands, and his sister waiting for an answer. "Yes," he said softly, his voice warm and meaningful. "Yes, I believe I do." And he lowered his lips to hers, kissing her much longer than he knew she would want, and reveling in that knowledge. "I forgot to do that at the courthouse," he said, explaining the kiss in a way April couldn't refute in front of Bri.

Her eyes snapped sparks at him, but he'd felt a slight response in her supple lips.

"Well, don't stand out there all night kissing her, Caleb," Bri said, laughing. "She's going to become the ice princess. Even though April looks like there's no place she'd rather be than on that porch with you. But come on, you two. There's time enough for that later."

April followed Bri inside, and he could almost feel the indignation in his bride as she stiffly walked, her knee-length, bell-shaped skirt snapping from side to side.

He was starting to think that warming up an ice princess might be challenging. He loved a challenge.

In the drawing room the whole clan waited until Caleb and April entered to erupt into approving applause. Astonished, April halted, so he took her hand in his to steady her. "Smile," he said. "We're in love."

"When you say it, I end up having to say it, so I wish you'd quit!" she complained under her breath.

"Were you a flop in high-school theater?" he asked, also under his breath as he nodded his thanks for his family's compliment to his bride.

Glasses of champagne were lifted high to them as a butler passed by offering April and Caleb a flute. Adam called out, "Here's to Mr. and Mrs. Caleb McCallum. May they be happy all their lives, and enjoy the fullest fruits of marriage!"

If April turned any redder, Caleb thought, she would match the berries in the Christmas holly. "You're cute when you're caught," he told her.

"You're annoying when you're full of yourself."

He lifted his flute, clinking hers. They drank at the same time. "Don't throw the glass," he said with a wink.

"At you?" she asked sweetly.

"Into the fireplace. If you want to throw something, we'll have a pillow fight later. In your house, where I'm going to walk in every night and call, 'Honey, I'm home!'"

"You're going to learn to love that futon," she said as he swung her into a dance when soft waltz music started.

But he didn't answer. Her waist was tiny in his

hand, and she was beautiful, and not afraid of his admittedly somewhat overbearing cop personality, and...despite all their squaring off of territory, he couldn't remember the last time he'd felt so happy.

That was the way he always wanted to remember this New Year's.

Happy.

JUST BEFORE the stroke of midnight, Bri pushed Caleb and April under the mistletoe, which had been hanging in the big den since before Christmas.

He playfully shooed Bri away. Then, knowing April was uncomfortable standing under the green-leafed token to encourage kissing while his family watched them, he said for April's ears alone, "Make a wish. A wish for the new year."

"I wish with all my heart that you find Jenny," she said quietly as he took her into his arms to the satisfied, happy laughter of his family. "Yours?"

"The same," he said, lowering his face to hers as his family counted, "Three, two, one! Happy New Year, everyone!"

The family began singing auld lang syne, crackers were pulled, kisses enthusiastically exchanged—and none of it registered to Caleb as he finally kissed April, his bride.

Bride for a while.

APRIL WAS EXHAUSTED, as Caleb had to be as well. It had been a fast week, and no doubt they were both still suffering the aftereffects of the tension of Matthew being missing, and then jumping into tonight's wedding.

The electricity that snapped between them constantly was wearing, too. Possibly she'd had too much champagne to drink as she tried to act the joyful new bride.

Caleb's kiss at the stroke of midnight had taken the last of her reserve of energy to protest. It felt so good when he kissed her. She didn't mind when he slipped his hand through hers and tugged her to the front door. His family tossed birdseed on them as she and Caleb ran to the car. Caleb helped April into the seat, then got in the driver's side and switched the car on to warm it.

"How about a honeymoon suite tonight?" he asked.

She looked at him, surprised.

Shrugging, he said, "Maybe it's a good compromise for us until we figure out what we're doing. I don't really look forward to a futon on my wedding night, even if tonight is 'just for looks.' Your sofa is fine, but..."

"A honeymoon suite just to sleep in?"

"Dad said he knew my brother and sister would ask where we intended to spend our honeymoon. Since we're not really having one, Dad fobbed them off with an excuse about our busy work schedules. Bri moaned that it wasn't very romantic, and that she couldn't bear the thought of us just going back to your house or my apartment after the wedding. Dad decided to try to put her mind at rest, and made reservations at a hotel just minutes outside of Austin as his wedding gift. I told you my sister has romantic rocks in her head,'' he said with a grin. ''But I think staying in a hotel tonight is probably a good idea, anyway.''

''Why?''

''I think it might be a good way to keep things from being awkward.''

April considered that, admitting to herself that she was feeling anxious about their partnership. Maybe she might be less so if she weren't so aware of Caleb as an attractive male—her senses tightened her body like wire every time he touched her. ''Well, it *would* save us from having to debate sleeping arrangements. We could even get separate rooms at the hotel. Bri would never know.'' She waited for his reaction to her offer, wondering if he was as apprehensive about tonight as she was. There were definite undercurrents of attraction between them— and it was probably best to try to ignore them.

''Okay,'' Caleb said. ''We'll take Dad up on his offer. And Bri said she and Adam loaded some wedding gifts in the trunk for us. We can open those later.''

''Definitely later.'' April turned her head to stare out the window, hiding her feelings of swift and startling disappointment. ''In fact, we should just save them so that your brother and sister can return them to the store after we get a divorce,'' she said, telling herself that was a rational plan.

''That's an idea.''

But April wasn't watching, so she missed the sudden worried look on Caleb's face.

TWENTY MINUTES LATER, April was awakened by Caleb saying her name. ''Nurse Sullivan-McCallum,'' he said in an official-sounding voice.

''Not funny,'' April replied, sitting up to tuck some wisps back into her upswept hair. ''For just a minute, I thought I'd fallen asleep at the hospital and you were a doctor who'd caught me dozing.''

''We're here. Let's go check in and I'll carry you to your room. But not over the threshold.''

''I can walk, but thank you for trying to be such a gentleman.'' She got out of the car, waiting for him to meet her. They hurried inside the lobby, going straight to the desk.

''We're Mr. and Mrs. Caleb McCallum,'' he told the desk clerk. ''We have a reservation.''

The clerk checked the computer. ''Ah. The honeymoon suite. Right away, sir.''

''We'd prefer two single rooms, if that's possible,'' April told the man, standing up on her toes so that she could see over the high, elaborate desk better.

The clerk eyed her wedding attire with a carefully studied glance. ''I'm sorry, ma'am. The conference

that's here has taken all the rooms except the honeymoon suite. You were lucky to get that.''

April sank back onto her heels. ''Oh, I see.''

''It's quite large,'' the desk clerk said suddenly,
his face noncommittal. ''I'm certain you'll find that
the spacious accommodations will suit your needs.''

She blushed, and Caleb took the key from the
helpful man. ''Thanks.'' He tucked it into his
pocket, took April by the hand to drag her across
the marble floor to the elevator, punched the button,
and when the doors opened, swept her up into his
arms and carried her into the elevator.

April could see the clerk staring over the counter,
his studied expression gone, his mouth wide open.

''Why did you do that?'' April demanded, staring
up at Caleb as her heart began a nervously thrilled
hammering.

''You said you couldn't be swept, carried or ravished. I have now swept you off your feet.'' The
doors brushed open, and he purposefully carried her
down the hall with long strides. ''I have now carried
you.''

''Caleb—'' April said, becoming slightly worried,
and even worse, somehow warm with desire. All her
tiredness and the calming lull of the champagne
were gone.

''But no ravishing,'' he said as he opened the
door to their suite. ''I'm trying to set your mind at
ease, because I can tell you're just about to jump
out of your skin with mistrust of me. That is, unless

your unease is because *you* prefer to do the ravishing?''

His hopeful tone broke the alarm she was feeling and made her laugh—as well as notice the twinge of regret she felt as he put out a hand, signaling for him to precede her into their suite. ''I'm not much for ravishing, myself. Sorry.'' But had the idea sounded kind of enticing to her love-starved ears?

''Wait a minute,'' he said, reaching out to snatch her back outside the door.

''What are you doing?'' she gasped, taken totally aback by his reversal.

''I've had a change of heart. Every bride, even a short-term, impostor bride, should be carried over the threshold. I'm sorry, but I have to stand by my convictions.'' He lifted her into his arms again, cradled her against his chest, held the door open with his foot and backed into the suite.

She gazed up at him silently.

He stared down at her, his eyebrow cocked. ''No protests?''

''I don't think so,'' she said, her voice tiny and somehow wondering. ''What would you say if I told you I liked it? Very much?''

Without another word, he laid her on the honeymoon bed. ''I'd say nothing at all. I might even take it as encouragement.''

They watched each other for a few seconds, April hesitating as she lay back, Caleb at her side, his arm crossed over her hip as he leaned on his hand for support. There was nothing in his eyes to be afraid of, she told herself. If she didn't know it was all a cover-up, she'd say that their wedding night couldn't have gone better. And she'd want it to last forever, if it was real.

Swallowing nervously, she said, ''I did like it very much.''

''I am taking that as encouragement,'' he told her, the warning there if she cared to heed it.

''I think that…I hope you do,'' she said, her heart in her throat, her whole body trembling with wonder.

Chapter Nine

Caleb's heart began a wild pounding in his chest. "I know that you don't love me, April, and that we're not long-term. I know I make you nervous, I could tell that at the desk downstairs. I don't want to frighten you in any way."

"I know," she said, her gaze on his, trusting.

"I would never hurt you."

Her eyelashes lowered for a split second before she said, "Tonight was the most beautiful night of my life. I wish it would never end, Caleb. But there's one thing I can't stop thinking about."

Caleb stroked her hair and then down along her neck. "Did you know white is sexy on you, whether it's part of a nurse's uniform or a wedding gown?"

"Caleb." She pecked lightly at his chest to hold his focus, and he realized his mind was in a far different place than hers. But what could he do? Everything about this petite woman made him want to hold her in his arms and shelter her from life.

"What is it, babe?" he asked huskily. "Tell me what you can't stop thinking about."

"I know nothing about you, really." She took a deep breath. "I know your family. I know that you're the son of the McCallum Wing's founder."

He couldn't stop the withdrawal from her, as much as he tried. It was in the cooling of his hands, and the stiffening of his spine. What she wanted was to get inside him, know him better than just a surface presentation to the world.

One thing he would never allow himself to do was pair himself so tightly to a human being that there was a bond, a sealing of spirits.

He looked into her earnest green eyes. Her need for emotional satisfaction was reasonable. Here they were, man and woman, husband and wife, without anything more between them than the reason they'd married. "I'm not trying to be mysterious. I just don't make it a habit to get close to people. Or to spill my guts."

"I know. It's just that..."

What she was thinking was in her eyes. Her body wanted his, the same way he wanted her, and yet, her mind asked for a connection to his soul. Nothing wrong with that. A different thing than he wanted from her, but the same, in the end, since he needed to protect her, keep her safe, and that was an emotional level she wasn't comfortable with him seeking. "Neither of us is right for the other," he said huskily. "We both want something the other can't give."

"I know that. I'm not completely innocent."

Touching her face, he enjoyed stroking the delicate skin. "I wonder if either of us could compromise."

"Probably not." She caught his hand and held it against her cheek. "Not enough, anyway."

"And yet I want you, April. More than anything I've ever wanted in my life." He turned the hand she pressed to her cheek, so that he carried her hand to his lips to kiss her palm.

"Nurses help people get well. You wouldn't have asked me to marry you if you weren't suffering, Caleb. It wasn't all about the children. Your actions told me it was also about making your father happy. Laying some demons to rest. You'll have to let me get to know you at some level, or I'll never know which shadows of yours you don't want disturbed."

If she wasn't a vision in angel-white lying on the hotel bed, he'd have been long gone by now. If they hadn't said vows—vows that meant nothing and yet reverberated inside him somehow—he'd have pulled a major disappearing act. Staring at April's sweet heart-shaped lips, meant for giving and receiving pleasure, stayed him. In a split second, a window in his mind opened. April had hit a salient point, whether she realized it or not: He wanted from her exactly what he did not know he wanted to be given.

Healing.

From screaming dreams in the night. From loneliness. From darkness.

The realization frightened him. This petite red-haired woman was too delicate to heal him. He'd take her under with him, just as a drowning victim might accidentally drown his rescuer. As a former cop, he knew better than to recklessly undercut his position.

He started to pull away. April swiftly put her arms around his neck, pulling him down to her, and before he could heed the warning, she'd touched her lips to his in a way that invited more intimacy.

Groaning, he gave himself up to her because he was tired of running away.

And because she was right. He did need to be healed.

APRIL HAD NEVER been kissed like this in her life. She melted into Caleb's arms, unwilling to give up the moment they were sharing. His tongue swept into her mouth, possessing her the way she'd once dreamed would happen for her; long strokes of need had her whimpering for more connection, more depth, more Caleb.

His hand stroked up her thigh, rasping on the white stockings. At the garter, he hesitated, and it seemed he took a shuddering breath as he investigated the skin encircled by the garter. Then he went to her lacy thong, pushing the full white skirt up as he sought the top of her thigh. She gasped, feeling as if she was going to fly apart if he didn't release her from the anguish her need was demanding.

"Caleb," she pleaded.

"No," he whispered, kissing her deeply again. "I can't rush this."

She arched underneath him as he kissed her neck, her earlobe, her collarbone. With unsteady fingers, she undid his tie, pulling it from his neck and dropping it to the floor. It was harder to undo his shirt buttons, and she sat up to push his jacket off of him.

He undid her zipper while he gnawed lightly on her neck. Shivers shot over her skin.

"Are you okay?" he asked against her earlobe.

"Yes," she said, her voice unsteady, her heart going crazy inside her. To show him she was, she pushed his shirt from his shoulders, helped him unbutton the cuffs and dropped that to the floor as well.

Bare-chested, he was breathtaking. The dark trousers emphasized a toned waist and an ebony trail of hair that led to the place she wanted to be.

She popped the fastener on his trousers, and he tugged her bridal gown off. His swift intake of breath told her he hadn't expected her to be braless. "The straps were so thin—"

His lips closed over her breast, cutting off her explanation and any chance she might have had to form a reason for refusal. Moaning, she clasped his head to her, sighing as he licked, nipped, suckled her. "Oh, Caleb. That feels *so* good. So *very* good."

She wanted him to feel pleasure, too, so bravely

she slipped a hand inside his trousers, inside his briefs, to massage him. For just a moment, her hand stilled as she considered his girth. He felt large, almost overwhelmingly so, and for just an instant she wondered how they would fit together.

"It's all right," he said, lying her back against the pillows. "Don't worry. I'll take care of you."

Standing, he removed his pants, and his socks and shoes. Last, his briefs. April's eyes grew wide as she stared at him. He was big all over, and more handsome than she could ever have dreamed.

She wanted to be beautiful for him. As attractive as she found him to be. Shyly, she found herself freezing into uncertainty. He seemed to sense her sudden hesitation, because he gently drew the bell-shaped gown over her hips and down her legs, tossing it onto a nearby wingback chair. His gaze drank in her bare breasts; his finger caressed a path from her waist to her hip where the white garter belt began.

"I knew you'd be beautiful, April, but I never dreamed you'd be this beautiful."

The words calmed her like a balm to her undernourished spirit. Gently, he removed her high-heel jewel-patterned shoes; he reached around her to unsnap the garter and take that and the stockings down, over her knees and down her ankles, so slowly she thought she might scream from the way he was staring at her.

There was nothing left but the thong. Caleb

seemed content to let his gaze rove from her pink-painted toenails to the cameo at her throat. To her lips, then back to her pink-tipped breasts. She wondered why he hesitated. "Caleb?" she asked, reaching out to touch his face.

"You're so much sweeter than I could have imagined," he said, his voice raw with emotion. "You're like a doll. I'd like to sit you up in my bed and look at you all night long."

His approval warmed her. "This doll would rather be held," she said. "I won't break."

It seemed a sigh of indecision left him. Whatever was battling inside him lay defeated, because ever so slowly, he reached for her white thong, and as carefully as if he were peeling petals from a rose, he took it down her legs.

Stroking lightly up her thighs, he seemed to admire her femininity, then suddenly his fingers teased inside her. She closed her eyes, swept by growing desire. When his tongue parted her, sliding inside her in a way she'd never expected, moving deeper to possess her, she grabbed his shoulders to hold on to him.

"Oh," she murmured. "Oh, Caleb!"

He sought her secrets with his tongue. "Caleb!" she cried out, feeling herself ride up on a giant wave that suddenly exploded. She felt a scream rising inside her, begging for something she couldn't understand, and then Caleb moved over her, parting her with his fingers as he eased inside her.

Tears of release began to spill from her eyes. "Yes," she told him, urging him with her hands. "Yes, yes, yes!"

"Come to me, baby, come to me," he patiently encouraged.

The building scream she'd been holding back erupted, pushed out of her by the uncontrollable pleasure driven by the shattering fire sweeping her, even more thrilling because his hoarse cries signaled his release was as passionate as hers.

"Don't leave me," she begged softly as he slumped against her, his lips against her shoulder in supine gratitude. "Stay inside me."

"Be careful," he said against her ear. "I could be easily tempted to stay inside you all night."

"Could you?" she whispered, thinking that would be nothing short of heaven.

"Oh, my, you are so sweet." He groaned and she thought it was a sound of pleasure. He turned, cradling her so that he stayed in her as she'd asked, and yet allowing him to lie more underneath her so that his weight was not on her.

She felt him kiss the top of her head, and for some reason, all the worry and tenseness left her body.

For the first time in her life, she felt sheltered. And whole.

MORNING CAME FASTER than April wanted. She was a morning person, always eager to greet the day.

Today, she just wanted to lie in Caleb's arms. Yet

that was not possible. Without disturbing him, she rose from the bed, showered, and changed back into her wedding dress. This time she didn't add the silk garter or stockings. Those she tucked into her purse. Her hair she pulled up into a knot, and then slipped her shoes on. It just didn't feel right to walk around wearing the same wedding finery she'd worn the night before. She wasn't truly a bride in the forever sense, and somehow, she felt a sham. The gorgeous wedding ring sparkled on her finger, a reminder that Caleb was a considerate gentleman, a man who would stand up and protect what he believed in.

The lovemaking had been so shattering and wonderful because she knew she could trust him, knew that his credo of "your cause is now my cause" had given her the security she'd needed. But she had so little to offer him in return.

When she came out of the bathroom, Caleb was dressed as well, but without his tie and jacket. His hair was rumpled, as if he'd run a hand through it. She couldn't believe she was married to such a devastatingly handsome, altogether-too-sexy man. Had he really held her in his arms last night, murmuring sweet words of passion she had never thought to hear said to her in her life?

"We look just a little different than we did last night," she said, her smile regretful for the night of passion that would never be theirs again.

His expression was rueful as well. "It was quite a night."

She didn't know how to take that, exactly. But she knew she'd reached out to him last night for shelter; he'd provided it. Now was the time to walk away gracefully, without putting more entanglements into the relationship than they had both agreed upon. Hadn't she been the one who'd been eager to set boundaries with which they'd both be comfortable?

"I'm anxious to get home and change and do some things so I can get to the hospital," she said softly.

"With it being New Year's Day," he said, "I'm curious to see if there are any teens hanging around the local hot spots, blowing off boredom."

So it was back to work, back to the normal routine for both of them. She nodded, knowing it was best if they both went on about their separate lives.

"Monday morning, we go put in the application for the quads," he told her. "Agreed?"

"Agreed. Definitely." She gave him an appreciative smile. "Thank you, Caleb."

He shrugged. "Nothing to thank me for. Yet."

There was, in so many ways she couldn't tell him. So she picked up her purse and waited for him to lead the way downstairs. He had his car brought around, and while they waited, April tried to ignore the cold wind whipping against her bare legs. Last night she'd been so warm.

Last night had been the most wonderful night of

her life. She wondered if Caleb had any idea just how much she'd needed him.

That was not the basis on which to start this partnership, she reminded herself. The need in the marriage was the quads', not her own personal yearnings. So she remained silent as they got in the car. She didn't say a word when he pulled the car in front of her house. No protest left her lips as he walked her to the porch, clearly having no intent to enter her house with her.

But after she opened the door and hesitated, not looking at him, and lost for words, he took the hand dangling at her side and raised it to his mouth. He pressed a kiss against her palm without lingering, a kiss that didn't seek more but was a gesture of chivalry.

Anything more would have spoiled what they'd shared, and what they both knew would not happen again. She offered him a tiny smile of understanding, and then murmured goodbye as she went inside and closed the door behind her.

A moment later, she heard Caleb's car pull away. A deep sigh of relief left her as she closed her eyes, remembering one more time what he'd given her. Then resolutely, she walked down the hall to her bedroom.

It was time to give up the past. There was not a doubt in her mind that she and Caleb had qualifications not even Social Services could ignore. He was the son of the wing's founder; he and his family were well known for their generosity. He had been a respected police officer. She was a neonatal nurse. There really was nothing now that Social Services could nitpick. Today, she felt certain that the quads would be awarded to them as soon as they could leave the hospital. Marrying Caleb had given her that reassurance.

So now she needed to make some changes. The babies could sleep in one of the guest rooms, or two in each guest room. The cribs and other paraphernalia would certainly fit very nicely.

Caleb couldn't always sleep on the sofa. She could easily move a bed for herself into one of the rooms where the children would be, thereby being able to keep close to them in the night. Caleb could use her room.

She went out to the garage and gathered up some boxes left over from when she'd moved into the house. Carrying them to her bedroom, she retrieved some packing tape and taped the boxes back into shape from their collapsed state. With one last glance around her room, she eyed the doll collection she had built over so many years. A beautiful ensemble, certainly, but nothing a man would want in his space. She wanted Caleb comfortable.

Without hesitating, she took the dolls, one by one wrapping them in tissue paper and storing them in the boxes. "Goodbye," she said as she carried the boxes to the garage. "Someday you'll mean a lot to someone. But I don't think Caleb will want to sleep every night with you watching over him.''

That vision made her laugh. It hadn't been so bad packing up her cherished memories. In a way, she felt as if she'd closed a door in her life. Where the dolls once had comforted her, now she had someone who comforted her in a much more tangible way. It was only for a short while, only until they found Jenny and got her resettled with her family—but for April, who had never known the depth of that support before, it was something she knew she'd never forget.

Chapter Ten

Monday morning, Caleb picked April up at her house. It was still her house, of course. That would never change. For a moment, the irony struck him. She was his wife, and yet, she wasn't.

A woman like her would be a real right angle chunked squarely into his neatly ordered life. He didn't want the emotions, the deep commitment, the abiding connection they would have to forge. The magic they'd allowed to sweep over them on their wedding night would never happen again. Neither of them would want it, for so many reasons.

So he put on his cop face, and gave her doorbell a serious stab with his finger. No way was he going to let his bride-for-a-while make him go all soft.

She came to the door wearing a lavender skirt and wool top, and sensible heels by no means old-fashioned, but by no means stiletto, either. Her hair was up, and she took his breath away faster than the cold breeze.

''Hello,'' she said, her voice quiet and unsure.

He knew exactly where her head was at. Despite their agreement, there was so much tugging between them that it was tempting to give in to the pull and go with it. See where it took him. "Hi," was all he said instead. "Got all the pertinent papers you'll need to satisfy the first round Social Services throws at us?"

Her smile was tremulous and apprehensive. "I hope so."

"Good." Taking her hand, he helped her down the porch. "Now remember, you and I have known each other for some time. That's not exactly a fib, because we knew of each other because of Bri."

"I feel like I've known you forever."

"Right. So we decided to get married. I don't think they'll be interested in the whys or wherefores of our relationship past that."

April was breathless as he helped her to his car. Nerves, he thought. "Don't be nervous," he said automatically. "We've got a great chance."

"Do you really think so?"

They got in the car, and he started it without looking at her. The less he maintained eye contact with those dazzling eyes of hers, the less likely he was to drown in her feelings. "You see anybody else lining up to take in four newborns?"

"No, but that doesn't mean there aren't. We don't know who might want them."

"I'm prepared to make the case that the mother's wishes should be considered, whether the document was legal or not. I'm willing to say that I'm working on the case, I believe I can find the mother, and it would greatly help if this grieving person who was little more than a child herself found that her family was taken care of in the manner she'd hoped. Even Social Services won't want to scare Jenny half to death by discovering that her babies were separated. Clearly, what she had in mind was giving them a family she felt she couldn't give them herself.''

"I hope you're right. And thank you for saying that you're willing to go to bat for me."

"I believe in my heart it's best for all concerned, or I wouldn't do it. I wouldn't have offered to...to—'' He couldn't finish, uncertain as to how to put his opinion without insulting her. She was his wife, after all.

"You wouldn't have offered your protection to us if you didn't believe it was the right thing to do. It makes me feel good that you trust me that much, Caleb.''

"Trust you?'' He turned to stare at her, forgetting all about his vow to keep himself from drowning in her gaze. "Anybody can see that you love those children, April. They need that right now.''

Her smile lit on him like a bright star. He felt a groan go through him. So he turned back to face the road, and reminded himself that April was a place he had vowed never to go again in his life. Partnership and caring. Being there for someone.

He told himself he was way too scarred to get lost in his heart again.

"Have you been able to find any leads on Jenny? Or have the police?"

That question centered him again, in a place where he was comfortable. The cop in him came strong to the fore. "I talked to some of her friends. Acquaintances, actually, but in the teen years, friendships are fairly liquid. They haven't seen her since she gave birth. That's a bad sign."

"Why? You don't think something's happened to her?"

"No," he reassured her. "I think she's not in the city any longer. Possibly not in the state. There had to have been someplace she had family."

"She never mentioned it to me."

"Someone somewhere knows what I need to know. It's simply a matter of patience until I knock on the right door and talk to the person with the golden key."

April rubbed her hands over her arms. "It's so hard to have that patience."

"I know. But I believe this case is by no means hopeless. I almost feel like we're holding all the cards. I can totally sympathize with what Jenny did."

"You can?" April's tone was astonished.

"Sure. She had a lot on her plate all at once. It was too much. Given time, she might even work through what happened, and want her children back without us having to encourage her to feel that way.''

''You really believe you're going to find her, don't you?''

''Yeah. Sure.'' He sent her a fast glance. ''I'll keep playing the angles over in my mind until something sticks out funny, and then it'll come to me.''

She was silent for a moment. ''One day, when you feel like it, I'd like you to tell me about your time on the force.''

That surprised him. It didn't surprise him that she'd want to know; women usually didn't have the caution not to try to push into his feelings. Like they could bind him up and cauterize the wound if they could only get him to talk about it. Well, his was a wound which couldn't be cauterized, so he never talked to anyone about it.

But the tone of April's voice wasn't intrusive. She seemed to really want to hear about his life. He caught no false sympathy, no egged-on encouragement in her voice.

Yet, he really didn't need to talk about it. His story was safely bottled up and stored where it couldn't come out and ooze into his life.

''I enjoyed being a police officer,'' he said, surprising himself. ''Being able to help people is something I find rewarding.''

''Me, too,'' April said, seemingly pleased that they shared this in common. ''I feel worthy, like I've found my reason to take up space on earth, when I'm helping other people. Especially people who really need to be helped."

That was what it was all about for him. "Exactly."

He intended to be no more forthcoming than that. Waiting for her to draw more out of him now that she'd hooked into an empathy scenario between them, he was surprised by her silence. He sensed her waiting, and also her patience. If he wanted to talk now, he could. If he didn't, he perceived she'd just return to looking out the window, understanding that he could only give to her when he had something to give.

Somehow, that noncondemning, nonwaiting silence encouraged him. "You know, I don't think I realized that we had something in common. I mean, something other than wanting the babies to have one home, one safe situation."

"What do you mean?" She turned inquisitive eyes upon him.

"I just think it must take a special woman to take care of babies who are so helpless that all they can do is trust. And the parents, who have to trust that you can make their children healthy. Not everyone can do it."

"Serving the public has its wrenching moments, as you know," she said carefully. "It also has its extremely rewarding moments."

Man, did this woman ever know how to say exactly what he'd always felt.

"And when something goes wrong, it's like…a sweeping loss you can't help feeling is your fault. I mean, you're the one everybody trusted, right? It was your job to be the best, to be the trustworthy savior."

Too close to home, he thought raggedly. This woman was reading his emotions. And yet, somehow, he wasn't as resentful as he'd expected he might be. "My partner was killed in a drug bust that went wrong."

She didn't reach to touch his hand. She merely said, "I'm so sorry, Caleb." Softly, with the right touch of shared commiseration. "And you believe you should have been the trustworthy savior."

"Right."

"Tell me something I couldn't guess on my own," she said, softly mimicking words he'd once spoken to her. "If not the details, then pretty much the story. But you know what fascinates me, Caleb? In spite of all that, here you are, willing to be the trustworthy savior once again. Just in a different capacity. And I really, truly admire that."

Nothing to admire about letting somebody down. But he had to smile at her refusal to coddle him. It annoyed him when people tried to understand his pain in their well-meaning manner. He hated it worse when they tried to give him advice.

April, perhaps true to form, did neither. She just offered him some sass and a little salute, and it added up to just what he needed.

"One day, maybe I'll be able to sleep at night. In the meantime, I'm not making any plans to move into your house until we have the babies. There's really no reason to do so."

"I couldn't agree more."

Well, it couldn't be said that she was after his body. He wondered if he should be irritated that she wasn't more enthusiastic about an encore performance of last night. "You're not the kind of girl to go all gooey on a guy about anything, are you?"

"I hope not. That sounds very unattractive."

Her teasing response took the last edge off his reserve with her. "I took it pretty hard when my partner died. I keep replaying that night, thinking of everything I did wrong. I just think I could have saved him if I'd been a better cop."

"Jenny might not have left if I'd been a better nurse. If I'd been paying closer attention to the signs. To her emotional condition."

He gaped at that logic, as much as he could clearly see the parallel she was drawing. "Do you really think that?"

"Yes." She shot him an impatient glance. "Is it not my job to be the one to pick up on the signals and make certain nothing goes wrong?"

"Yeah, but—"

"There's no buts for me, just like there aren't for you. And the worst part is, I don't know if Jenny's dead or alive."

"She's alive."

"She was not a healthy patient when she left the hospital. Anything could have happened to her."

An infection just by itself could zap a woman off the earth quicker than anyone could figure out the cure... A shudder shook him. They'd reached the offices of Social Services, so he parked and switched off the engine. "I think you're good to talk to. For the first time, I feel like someone knows what it's really like to be on the front line."

Her gaze was even. "It doesn't solve anything for either of us. We still have all the baggage."

"Yeah, but the compartments just shifted. Maybe, eventually, we'll just lose the baggage, kind of like the airports lose it."

Rolling her eyes at him, she said, "Come on. We've got babies to safeguard."

So they got out of the car, and he grabbed her hand, her soft, delicate hand that hid a gentle touch and a strong heart. The weird thing was, he didn't mind rushing to April's side to try to shore her up. He believed in her, the way she believed in him.

And that felt strangely nice.

In a nonpermanent sort of way, he reminded himself as they walked through the doors into the Social Services offices.

TWO HOURS LATER, April and Caleb were finished with the initial paperwork, and the questions she was so afraid she'd answer wrong. It had been draining. Wrenching. And somehow, painful.

"Are you okay?" Caleb asked when they left the building to get into his car.

"I'll feel better when we know if they're taking us seriously as candidates."

"It's going to be okay. I just know it. Do you want to get a bite to eat at Austin Eats? You could go right in to the hospital after that."

"You know, I don't think I feel like seeing a whole bunch of people right now, and there'll probably be a lot of staff hanging around, catching up after the holiday. I think I'd like to go get my car, Caleb, so you won't have to pick me up when I'm ready to leave the hospital."

"All right. I need to go by and see Dad anyway. He's going to want to hear about how our meeting with Social Services went."

"Tell him I said thank you for the honeymoon suite."

Caleb gave her leg a quick pat as he drove. "I have to say I enjoyed it a lot myself."

She stared out the window, wondering if there was a double meaning in his words.

"By the way, I went by and saw Mrs. Fox yesterday."

"You did?"

"Yeah. She was actually pretty happy to have company on New Year's Day."

"Oh," April murmured. "I guess she might have enjoyed not being alone. It's got to be quiet without Jenny around."

"She's a pretty nice lady. I can see why Jenny leaned on her after David died. But she didn't have a whole lot of details on Jenny's history, besides the fact that she was really grieving for her husband. Mrs. Fox said she didn't think Jenny might ever get over losing him, and that she was frightened to death of having four children on her own."

"Oh, dear." April could imagine the level of deep grief herself. It had to have been so overwhelming for a teenager without family.

Just walking into Social Services and doing paperwork to temporarily foster the quads had nearly panicked her. Knowing that someone had filled out paperwork on her when she was a child—actually, many people—had given her a nearly physical pain in her stomach. The process seemed so cold, and yet it had to be straightforward and nonemotional. Yet there were people's lives involved, and children.

As an orphan herself, Jenny would have understood what she was doing if she abandoned the children to the system. And yet, her own situation was intolerable. April might have been the only person she felt might understand.

"I think I mentioned to Jenny once that I had been in foster care," she said suddenly. "And that I'd been adopted."

He nodded. "It's really not too hard to figure out. I believe that she realized you were the only person who might understand her panic over her children not going into the foster care system. You and Jenny shared a similar belief system, a common background. Just like you and I have discovered something common between us.''

She stared at him, stunned by his admission. It was almost as if he was saying that they had achieved some level of closeness. Why did that shock her? ''I don't think I ever expected you to...I mean, that sounded so—''

He grinned at her loss of words. ''So hurray-for-the-home-team? Maybe I have to think of our relationship in terms of sports.''

''Oh.''

''That's the spirit. Now I'm going to do a few things today, but you call me if you hear anything, or need anything.''

''Okay.''

He parked the car at her house and April started to get out, halting when he caught her hand.

''I mean it, April. Call me if you need *anything*.''

The look in his eyes was deep and purposeful. He really meant that he would take care of her, in any way she needed, while they were married.

It was so wonderful to know that he wanted to be there for her—and it was so scary to find herself wanting to rely on him. Every other time a boyfriend in her life had wanted to let her rely on him, she'd taken off like a shot. Bonds had not been easy for her to form.

She felt one forming with Caleb, whether she wanted it to or not, and yet, she found herself drawn to it like a sunflower to the sun. *I could fall in love with him,* she realized faster than a blinking eye. *I like being married to him.*

That shocked her more than anything. Managing a quick smile for goodbye, she got out of the car and hurried up the sidewalk, letting herself into the house without another look back at him. Her heart thundered.

"What was I thinking?" she asked herself. "This will be over one day. And it's going to hurt so much more than being passed over at the orphanage when I have to face that Caleb doesn't want to stay married to me."

The dawning of her feelings for him were outside their agreement. She couldn't have foreseen that she'd begin to feel this way. There was so much good wrapped up in Caleb. Him. His family. His beliefs. Their mutual understanding. His lovemaking, and the way he treated her so gently.

It was balm to her spirit; it was a magnet pulling her heart inexorably toward his.

Nothing about this was going to feel good when it was gone from her.

Chapter Eleven

"So how's the newlywed?" Bri asked when April came in to check on the babies.

"I'm fine. Better than fine."

They hugged each other, reveling in the knowledge that they were sisters now.

"I'm only here for a quick visit, but my brother treats you good?" Bri asked.

A blush stole over April's cheeks. "Your brother treats me better than good."

"Oh my gosh," Bri said in wonder, her eyes not missing a detail of the glow in April's eyes. "You didn't say anything about how you and Caleb had decided to make the big leap. But you really like my crazy brother, don't you?"

April laughed. "He's not crazy."

"No, but he can be tough as old rawhide. Yet, the way you're smiling tells me you really like him. It all happened so fast I thought...well, I don't know what I thought. But there's something special between you two, I can see it in your eyes." She hugged April again, close.

"He hasn't been tough as rawhide with me. I couldn't ask for better." That was the truth, considering the circumstances, and it was painful to admit it, and to keep up the pretense even though she knew her marriage to Bri's brother wasn't forever.

"Did you enjoy the honeymoon suite?" Bri's eyes sparkled with some teasing, and some womanly interest as well.

April shifted, mildly embarrassed. "Thank you for suggesting it to Jackson. It was very sweet of you," she said, trying to sidestep the question.

Bri laughed. "Okay, it's none of my business. But you look happy, and glowing, and I take that to mean you enjoyed more about the suite than the accommodations."

Even with her best friend, this was almost more than she could share about Caleb and herself. "It was a lovely suite," she said primly. "I'm going to go check on the babies now."

"They've been in good hands, April. And they're getting stronger every minute. Though they will require constant care for a long time." Bri smiled at her, content to let wedding matters and honeymoon suites go for the moment. "Before you go, I do want to tell you how happy you made my father. He's thrilled that you're part of the family, April. I think Dad was always afraid Caleb would bring home a woman Dad wouldn't be able to relate to."

"Why?"

Bri shrugged. "It's the radical element in Caleb. He's different from the rest of us. His feelings are in a deep dark place. But Dad thinks you're wonderful, and that you're going to be great for Caleb. All that sweetness is bound to rub off on him somehow. Anyway, it's wonderful to have someone in the family who's blissful. My brother, Adam, and his wife, Maggie, are at the other end of the marriage spectrum. Not that they don't love each other, but they've been praying for a child of their own for so long. Fertility treatments have been unsuccessful so far, and it's all beginning to take a toll on them. I'd like to see them happy together again. Like you and Caleb. I'm telling you the truth, Dad was the happiest man at the wedding yesterday."

April didn't answer, not certain how to reply. Clearly, Jackson had spun their relationship to the family as a love match. She offered Bri a shy smile and a nod before making an excuse and hurrying down to the nursery.

"Oh, you little sweethearts," April murmured as she went to stand beside their isolettes. "You'll never guess where I've just been. Soon, I hope you'll be coming home with me. We'll find your mother, and we'll help her get started with you. And just you wait until you meet your temporary father. You're going to like him, because he's a special man."

As she touched the delicate toes and baby skin

she had come to love, April allowed herself to be-come lost in a hazy daydream. *If only these were my babies, and yet, my heart so wishes for their real mother to return.*

But still, I do love them as if they are my very own.

"Hi, April."

Her head snapped up as the daydream was snatched away. "Hi, Madeline," she said.

Madeline Sheppard smiled at her. "I wanted to come by and give my good friend my best wishes. Congratulations on your marriage."

"Oh. Thank you." April's face warmed as she realized her "happy" news would have spread throughout the hospital, fairly shouted by her exuberant sister-in-law.

"Bri is ecstatic that you're part of her family now."

"I am, too."

Madeline touched a few baby toes as she smiled wistfully. "My biological clock is ticking so loud it sounds like it might detonate any minute."

Madeline was a fertility specialist, and maybe for that reason, April had never thought of her as lacking anything where babies were concerned. And yet, Madeline had to think about babies all day long as part of her job—it was only natural to want the same for herself that she tried to help other couples achieve.

"I'm approaching a ripe old thirty-five in a few

weeks. If I had my way about it, I'd be married and expecting my own child by my next birthday. That's what I'm going to wish for when I blow out the candles on this cake, anyway.''

April smiled at her. ''I'll cross my fingers for you, too. Your prince could always be closer than you think, maybe just a wish away.''

''Yours certainly appeared from out of the mists. I thought all you ever did was work. Of course, now we all know you found a little time for romance,'' she teased.

April blushed. ''Caleb kind of…swept me off my feet.''

''Well, you seem so happy. Congratulations. Oh, I wish I could stay and hear all about it, but I've got to get back to work.''

''Thanks for stopping by, Madeline.''

Madeline left the room, and once again April turned to consider the infants. It would be so wonderful to have children of her own. She wasn't that different from Madeline. Actually similar, because she had no man with whom to become a partner in pregnancy. Caleb was temporary. No other man had suited her as either husband or father-to-her-children material.

It seemed almost too ironic to accept congratulations from Madeline when there was nothing to celebrate. ''Oh, well,'' she told the babies, ''for now, I've got you to hold, and who knows, that prince might be just a wish away for me as well.''

JUST AS A MATTER OF COURSE, Caleb decided to leave no stone unturned when it came to idle conversation. Someone had talked to Jenny and had heard something they didn't realize. The trick was finding out who had the information he needed.

He'd already tried the teen scene. Speaking with Mrs. Fox had been illuminating, but not necessarily the gold mine of clues he wanted. "Next stop, hospital staff," he said under his breath.

He caught Madeline Sheppard in the hall as she was leaving the neonatal nursery. "I'm Caleb McCallum," he said.

"Oh, the handsome groom who nabbed our sweet nurse. Bri can't stop doing cartwheels over your marriage."

"Bri's a romantic, but thanks." Caleb grinned, then got down to business. "Madeline, did you ever talk to Jenny, the mother of those quads in the nursery?"

"Once, maybe." Madeline's forehead creased. "I'm a fertility specialist, so I didn't have much reason to talk to her. She'd already hit more of the jackpot than most people ever do in their lives. But I did stop in once to say congratulations."

"So she never mentioned anything to you of a personal nature?"

Madeline smiled. "All she did was lie there. She could barely smile. When I saw Jenny, she was pretty exhausted from the delivery. I don't think she said a word, as a matter of fact."

Caleb nodded. "I can understand that."

"You might try her obstetrician," Madeline offered. "Zachary Beaumont delivered the quads."

"Thanks. I will."

"Congrats." Madeline gave him a friendly smile and walked away.

April came out in the hall, her eyebrows raised. "I thought I heard your voice. Are you flirting with the single women on the staff?"

"No. I'm kissing married ones." And he reached out and swiped her close to him, laying a big kiss on her lips.

She jumped out of his arms as if she'd been snapped. "Caleb!"

He laughed at her. "I can do that. We're married."

She visibly relaxed. "I forgot. I'm sorry."

His expression turned serious, though it was clear he was teasing. "We have to keep up appearances, you know."

"Of course. Well, goodbye."

She scurried back into the nursery as fast as her little white shoes could take her. Caleb laughed under his breath. She was so cute when she was unsettled. It served her right for teasing him about flirting. He wasn't a flirting kind of guy, and she knew it. That would be the last time she asked a question like that, because she knew what his answer would be.

A big smooch, where anybody could see.

He had really enjoyed that.

TEN MINUTES LATER, Zachary Beaumont gave Caleb a benign glance. ''I really didn't know Jenny Barrows very long. She was here at the hospital for a couple of weeks because having quadruplets requires special care, of course. But two weeks isn't long enough to know much about a patient.''

Caleb hated turning up big fat zeroes.

''She was a stellar patient, though. I'm surprised she left the way she did. The way she acted about those children, oohing and aahing over each of them as they were born, I thought she was more smitten than scared.''

''It was a lot of personal stuff, I think. Thanks, Doctor.''

''You're welcome. If anything else comes to mind, I'll let you know.''

''Thanks.'' Caleb headed off, deciding he'd go by his father's offices and talk with him. By now, he wondered why his father hadn't called him for a full report.

Of course, he might be less anxious for a report on the case now that he and April were married and applying for temporary custody. Caleb snorted to himself. No doubt Jackson hoped Jenny would stay gone long enough for he and April to figure out that they actually liked sharing residential square footage. Liked being married.

Wouldn't Jackson be surprised when he learned that Caleb and April maintained separate quarters and would continue to do so, at least until the babies went home with April?

JACKSON LOOKED at him from under beetled brows. "So the first round of paperwork at Social Services went fine?"

Caleb shrugged. "As far as we can tell. They keep their cards pretty close to the vest. Still, the babies may be able to go home soon. They'll have to go somewhere, and April and I are a ready-made family who can give them the constant care they require."

Jackson nodded. "How does it feel to be married?"

"Better than I thought it would." Caleb sent his father a sheepish glance. "Maybe I feel okay about it because I know that there's a timed release in it."

His father shook his head. "Well, you seem to like that little gal. Don't be in too big a hurry to push the destruct button. Great women are real tough to find."

"Don't I know it." Caleb rubbed a palm over his chin, ready to be off the subject. "I'm having no luck finding Jenny Barrows."

"That's unusual for you. Bloodhounds don't do any better at tracking scent than you do at putting missing pieces together."

Caleb frowned. "I know. I'm missing a huge piece, and it's bugging me. Teenagers don't disappear without a trace, especially when they have no money, no family and no resources. There had to have been someone she talked to.''

"I bet you stumble on it soon enough. You ate your black-eyed peas on New Year's, didn't you?''

"Don't tell me that superstitious tale of eating peas for luck is going to help me find Jenny.''

"No. I'm just asking you in a roundabout way if you and April cooked, or if you went out after your honeymoon.''

"We actually went our separate ways. She went to the hospital and I went to chat with local teenagers.''

Jackson grunted. "I take it the honeymoon wasn't a sufficient lure to keep you two together then.''

"Dad,'' Caleb said, his tone no-nonsense. "Don't try to make a romance where there isn't going to be one.''

"All right.'' Jackson sighed. "But damn, I like that little girl.''

"I know you do.'' Caleb sighed. "But I gotta like being married. And she's got to like it. Believe it or not, I'm not the only reluctant mule in the marriage.''

"Oh, I believe it, all right. That young lady's full of sass. Say, did she ever ask you about the prenup?''

"No. It was just as you said. She'd made her point, knows we accepted it, and beyond that, I don't guess the details interest her.''

"I sure do appreciate honesty and a good, hard-working stubborn streak in a woman," Jackson said wistfully. "April reminds me so much of—"

"Dad. I'm not going there." He stood, clapping a strong hand on his father's shoulder. "Thanks for everything you did to help us and to make things nice for the wedding. I've got to get back to work."

"You do that. Thanks for stopping by."

Caleb nodded, seeing the lines around his father's eyes and the concerned fold to his lips. "It's going to be fine, Dad," he said soothingly. "Don't worry."

"I'm not so old that you need to start parenting me," Jackson said, uncharacteristically petulant. "I've been around the track enough to know that everything eventually works itself out."

Caleb laughed at his dad's who-is-in-control-here tone. "That's my dad. Bye."

"Bye." Jackson waved him away, watching as his son walked out the office doors. Great gravy, was that any way to start a marriage, staying apart from one another? What would it take to get these two stubborn kids in one place long enough that they had to begin to work within the boundaries of the marriage agreement they'd made? Life was way too short to be so damn mule-headed.

And yet, as much as he wanted to wave his hand like an all-powerful genie to cast the proper spell that would make April and Caleb want to be husband and wife, he knew that wasn't the way marriage worked.

It took mutual craving.

There was no way to kickstart a craving.

He'd done his best, and he'd have to be satisfied with that. The rest was up to Caleb and April. Maggie and Adam. Bri and Hunter.

"You'd think, Emily," he said to his deceased wife, "you'd think that any man who dedicated a wing of a hospital to multiple births would get tons of grandkids. Adam and Maggie, I just don't know what to say about that except that I wish you were here to talk to your son and comfort his wife. Caleb's so ornery you might as well forget about any bundles of joy coming from that son of yours. Bri's coming along fine with her three, but it sure would be nice if her brothers would join in the fun and have a few kids of their own." He sighed deeply, his soul lonely. "You'd know what to say to these kids of yours. I miss you, woman, I truly do."

Chapter Twelve

After four weeks of interviews, visits to April's home and countless questions of their family members and work associates, a miracle happened. April and Caleb were allowed to take the four babies home for temporary foster care.

The moment April learned the news, she shrieked with joy she never really thought she'd get to feel. After that, everything happened fast. All the things that had been bought for the babies by Bri were taken to April's house. A minishower was given by Cherilyn, much like a shower for a woman expecting her very own child. Since this foster situation was temporary, there was a twist to the gifts. There was something small for use with the babies, like a set of washcloths with little ducks from each nurse—but then there was something for April from each friend as well. Lovely, breathtakingly sheer webs of lacy lingerie.

"You got married so quickly we didn't get you wedding gifts," Cherilyn explained. "And you won't have the babies forever, so we didn't buy any clothes for them past the six-month size. But your marriage to Caleb calls for something to keep that hunk right by your side,'' she teased.

So April ended up opening up beautifully wrapped gift after gift of lingerie, tasteful and exquisite. Meant to make a man look. And touch.

Of course, her friends had no way of knowing that the marriage was meant to be more short-term than the foster care.

The party was given for her on the last day of her employment, as she was taking an unspecified leave of absence until the babies were no longer in her care. The nurses and some of the doctors threw confetti at her and Caleb as they left with the babies, followed in a car by Jackson and Bri, who were coming to help move them in.

It almost felt like a real homecoming day. It was more than April had begun to believe could happen.

She carried Matthew's carrier inside her house, nearly trembling with excitement. Caleb carried in Craig, Bri brought in Melissa, and Jackson, who couldn't bear to be left out, carried Chloe in as if she were a fragile piece of china.

''An instant family, that's for certain,'' Bri said as they all took a baby to diaper and get changed for bed. ''You've decorated their rooms beautifully, April.''

Too distracted by all the excitement, April barely heard Bri's compliment. But she was glad that her sister-in-law thought the nurseries were suitable for the babies. On the days when she'd been off, she had decided to paint bright yellow colors on the walls in both bedrooms. She'd found huge cutouts of the moon, the stars, and even a castle, decorations that she realized the infants couldn't focus on yet, but during the waiting days, as she'd called them, the busywork kept her mind relaxed.

She'd even sewn tiny bumper rails. That had been a challenge, and after that project, decided she'd done enough and was just going to drive herself crazy.

She and Caleb hadn't seen each other much. He came by every once in a while with a pizza or other food item, making sure she ate. He'd help her paint, or hang the big cutouts, change some lightbulbs or help her with drapery rods, but beyond that, they didn't share affection. It was as if their wedding-night lovemaking had never occurred.

He seemed as content with that as she did. She couldn't have asked for more in a partner, because he seemed to understand that she needed to throw every ounce of her energy into what she called nesting. In a way, she felt almost expectant herself, as if she was simply waiting for her own day of giving birth.

Of course it was a silly fancy, but he didn't seem to think so. And once she'd shared that idea with him, he'd gone out and bought two sliding rockers, one for each room.

April had been delighted with the gifts. "You didn't have to do that, Caleb. But thank you!"

"We're going to need them for those all-night feedings. I figure the chances of four babies sleeping through the night is about nil."

He'd grinned at her, his hair rumpled from carrying the rockers in with a cold breeze blowing outside. The chill had touched his cheeks with a healthy ruddiness, and his eyes glowed even brighter. She liked him in jeans—too well—and the blue-and-black flannel shirt gave him a rugged appeal she couldn't help admiring.

Their lovemaking flashed into her mind, and April felt need warm her body. Attraction like she'd never known sped into her.

But that was outside what they'd agreed upon, and a sure way to destroy a good friendship. Because after this time in their lives was over, and Jenny was found and reunited with her children, what would she and Caleb have together?

Nothing but an agreement to wed for the sake of four tiny babies who would no longer be in their care.

But for now, the babies were here, and she had to focus on the short time they might have them. "Thank you," she said quietly to Caleb after he'd secured one baby in its crib. "You've been a wonderful partner."

"It's okay." He tugged at a long curl of her hair.

"I haven't done anything I haven't wanted to, babe."

"This little baby wants something, and I can't figure out what," Jackson said gruffly, coming in from the other nursery room, carrying a squalling Chloe in his arms. "You'd think after three of my own, I'd know what I was doing."

Bri laughed, coming to take the fitful baby from her father. "Not necessarily, Dad. Babies are puzzles sometimes. And crying is not always a bad thing. She may know she's been moved from her secure environment and feeling out of sorts. Or she could just be tired."

April smiled as Bri expertly checked Chloe over, trying a bottle and a fresh diaper. Then Bri placed the infant in a crib, and covered her with a warm blanket. Bri rubbed the baby's arms and legs and back soothingly, and Chloe finally allowed herself to relax.

They turned the Peter Rabbit lamp on, switched off the overhead light, and April picked up the baby monitor as they left the room.

"Good job, everyone," Jackson said, sinking into the sofa as they filed into the den. "I'd call that a successful transition. And I'm exhausted."

"Caleb, get your father a glass of tea from the kitchen, please," April said, smiling at her father-in-law fondly. No one could have tried harder to be a real part of the newly growing family than Jackson. In fact, she'd heard from Bri that Jackson might have placed a few calls to Social Services, offering them badly-needed diapers and formula donations and anything else he could do to help.

"It wasn't bribery," Bri had explained to April with a shrug. "Dad had the McCallum Wing finished, operating and out of his hands. Your struggle to win emergency custody of the quads gave him a new mission. He'd made a call to see if there was anything he could do, got to talking to Mandy Cole, realized there were needs as with any agency, and that gave him a new goal. He said Emily told him it was the right thing to do." Bri smiled at her sister-in-law with some sympathetic exasperation. "Emily was our mom."

"Yes, I know," April murmured. "Bless Jackson's heart."

"Oh, he talks a pitiful game. But behind that I'm-dying-until-I-have-my-own-grandchildren exterior is a man who's pretty content with life. He's got us all married, three grandchildren, four temporary babies to love and daily communiqués with Mother. He just likes to keep us all feeling like we could do a little more to make his golden years extra-shiny golden."

April had laughed, but now as she looked at Jackson on the sofa, she saw a man who simply loved his family. Adam, Bri and Caleb had been so fortunate to have Jackson for a father. Whatever bonds he hadn't been able to form with them as children, he seemed eager to tie now.

She wondered if Caleb had the same latent seed

of bonding in him. He'd said he didn't want to get close to anyone, but did he have the same capacity for allowing himself to heal and move on that Jackson possessed?

"Thank you for all your help," she said to Jackson, leaning over the sofa back to hug his neck. "It's meant an awful lot to me."

He caught one of her hands in his. "Not as much as it's meant to me, my girl," he said, his voice tight with emotion.

She couldn't help herself. After all the years of wanting a family of her own as much as she had, she felt so blessed to have the McCallums embrace her with open arms. Pressing a kiss to Jackson's cheek, he held her head against him for just a split second. "Thank you," she murmured.

"You're welcome," he whispered back.

Straightening, she caught Caleb staring at her, watching the exchange. To her surprise, he had a baffled expression on his face.

Almost as if he was perplexed by the affection that they shared.

CALEB WATCHED APRIL with his father, and with some surprise—and a lot of consternation—he realized that she loved his old man. Not just loved him, but wanted him to be happy. Appreciated him.

Why he should find this disturbing, he wasn't certain. He laid the glass of tea she'd requested for Jackson on the coffee table in front of him, glancing up to see his father watching him with some approval and gratitude.

"Thanks, son," Jackson said.

Caleb nodded, never very comfortable in anything but the role of renegade son. But that need seemed to be falling away from him more and more these days, and it was a direct result of April being in his life, he realized. With April, he found approval in his father's eyes. Because of her, he'd found a way to give his father exactly what he wanted—family, most especially a second chance to enjoy a large family—and yet Caleb hadn't had to do a damn thing. Put forth little effort and almost no emotion. April required no true love, no lasting commitment. Zippo. All he had to do was treat her the way he'd treat any woman, with respect and caring, and marry her for the length of time she needed, and he'd won the jackpot of instant "good" rapport with the old man.

The lovemaking had been a helluva bonus, of course.

But other than that, he could skip the emotional connecting he so wanted to avoid, paste a temporary wife and four babies onto the cardboard cutout of his life, and faster than he could say, "Look, Dad, no hands!" he'd won his father's respect and love.

Damn. Life didn't really work out that easy, did it?

April smiled at him, a soft glow of happiness and joy on her face, and his stomach sank. He wasn't supposed to feel pride when he looked at her. He wasn't supposed to feel attraction when she carried the babies, nor when she bent over to change diapers. He wasn't supposed to go into a soft, droopy daydream when she fed them a bottle, rocking them to sleep with a contented hum under her breath. He wasn't supposed to want to hold her in his arms at night and kiss her neck until she turned to him with the same want he felt burning him.

Life wasn't easy at all.

He had a feeling it was going to get more difficult.

AFTER HIS SISTER and his father left, the closest emotion he could remember since his partner's death swept over him.

Panic. Sheer raw panic.

He was alone with four babies and a woman, and they needed to become a family.

For the first time in his life, he truly realized how his father must have felt after his mother had died. He had no idea how to proceed. The flight instinct pushed at him surprisingly hard.

"You get Melissa," April said, "and I'll get Matthew. The others will lie quietly for a moment, but these two are a little more rambunctious when they wake up from their nap."

He did as she asked, mainly because courage was required at this moment, and if there was anything he could call up instantly when needed, it was courage. Cop training. He approached Melissa as if she were a time bomb. Gently, precisely, carefully. "Now, you and I are going to do this successfully," he told the tiny baby. "Because there's no one here anymore to hold our hand and bail us out. It's just me and you, babe, so let's make it good."

Melissa, unimpressed with his offer, let out a squall that seemed as loud to him as detonation. "Now, don't take that attitude," he told her. "I know you don't recognize my hands on your little body, but I assure you, I'm very gentle," he said soothingly. It didn't really matter what he said to her, did it, as long as he said it with baby-pleasing tones?

Unconvinced, she tore loose a greater shout, her little tongue curling into a tiny disk in her mouth. "My goodness," he said in the same quiet voice as he carried her over to the rocker. "You *are* a noisy young lady. If your daddy was here right now, he'd be so proud to know he had given life to either a cheerleader or a carnival barker."

She was unappeased, and disinterested in the bottle he offered her. "All right, young lady. If you have something else on your mind, why don't you let me know."

Melissa cried louder.

"Okay, I think I got the general consensus of the complaint you're lodging."

He heard a scraping sound in the hall and poked his head into the hallway. April was dragging the rocker across to the girls' nursery. "What are you doing?" he demanded.

"I think it was a mistake to separate the children while they're still so young," she said, breathless from trying to tug and push the heavy rocker while she held Matthew. "They're used to sleeping side by side in clear isolettes where they can see each other."

Baloney. Those babies couldn't see each other worth flip, he'd be willing to bet. April wanted to see him—and make certain he was doing his job right. Obviously, Melissa's forlorn attempts at a college-size yell were causing her new mom some angst, rather like a mother bear who hears her newborn cub yelping and rushes to the rescue.

"Hang on," he said to Melissa over her din. "Your mom is showing some anxiety. You crying is making her think she has to come in here to monitor me."

But he went out, picked up the rocker and carried it into the girls' nursery, the one with the castle on the wall, so that he and April could sit across from each other. He decided it might be best to show April that he knew exactly what he was doing.

"I think she wants her diaper changed," he said over Melissa's cries. "I am particularly adept at this."

"I'll just bet you are," April said, her eyebrows raised. "Don't you want me to do it?"

"I said I am an expert at this," he explained

loudly. "In crisis situations, particularly where a perpetrator is resisting, I like to perform what I call the sneak attack. Watch closely."

Gently, he turned the baby on her back and laid her in the crib. "Now, most women don't complain about this part, but I sense you're going to show me you're different, so it's going to be over before you know what happened, sweetie." Deftly, he undid the tapes, tossed the diaper aside, scooted a new one underneath the baby, gave her a couple of quick swipes with a diaper wipe and taped the new one in place, before picking her up to snuggle her against his chest—all in under fifteen seconds.

"And that, little one, is a sneak attack. It's best if you know about such maneuvers on the part of the male species so you can fend them off later." Sitting down in the rocker across from April, he said, "Don't you have anything you want to say? Questions? Comments? Praise?"

"I do have a question. Is the sneak-attack part of the cop manual, or just yours?"

He grinned at her, calming the now-almost-still Melissa with the warmth of his arms. "Are you asking out of professional curiosity, a need to learn my diapering skills or a desire to experience my sneak attack?"

Chapter Thirteen

Well, Bri had once mentioned that Caleb was fairly confident with his appeal to the opposite sex. Not interested, just confident. And he'd already shown her that he could back up his confidence, April thought with a warming of her female anatomy.

He was suggesting none too bashfully that he could have her panties off before she knew it—and that she wouldn't even protest.

He was right.

How she'd *love* to wipe that smug grin off his face.

Melissa did it for her, burping up a giant bubble of formula all over his shirt. "Oops, I think I hear Craig waking," she said, scooting swiftly from the rocker. "You've already proved you're equipped to deal with all female emergencies and otherwise, so I'll leave you to it."

And she hurried from the room, cherishing the surprised and somehow appalled expression on Caleb's face. "Well, he deserved it," she said, snuggling her face against Matthew's warm neck. "I'll leave him with Chloe and Melissa, since he thinks he's got all the know-how when it comes to sugar-and-spice-and-everything-nice. I'll settle for snips-and-snails-and-puppy-dog-tails, not that I can claim to have his experience with the opposite sex, but just because it's good for him to recognize that sneak attacks on a female might give him unexpected results, like Melissa's sneak attack on *him*."

Matthew didn't seem to care about the battle of the sexes, though, as he allowed her to slip him into his crib. Slowly, she drew a blanket over him, then went to check on Craig. Though she'd pretended she heard him crying, the baby slept peacefully.

She might not have this much quiet again for a while. With Caleb here to take care of Melissa and Chloe—and keep an ear out for the other two—she decided to shower and change. Creeping from the room, she peered into the girls' nursery.

Caleb had his back turned to her. The babies were safe in their cribs, and he had just finished pulling off the offensive shirt. She held back an instant gasp. Broad and strong, his muscular back tapered into a trim waist. A thick leather belt corded through the blue-jeans loops. His feet were bare, as if he was planning to...he reached to his front, and she realized he was undoing his belt buckle. Those jeans were about to come off, and it didn't matter that she'd lain in his arms one night enjoying more bliss than she ever thought possible. She hadn't seen him up close and personal in fairly good light, and as much as she secretly might want to see him in the raw, she simply couldn't. She fled, heading into the bathroom and quietly closing the door so that he wouldn't know she'd passed down the hall.

"Okay," she said, her heart beating hard in her chest. "Rule number one of communal living. We don't take off clothes unless the door is closed. Maybe we need a bell. Something to alert the other person that clothes are about to be shed." No, not after Caleb's sneak-attack theory. She had a funny feeling ringing a bell when she was about to undress could cause a Pavlov's-bell type of reaction.

The door to the bathroom suddenly opened, and April gasped, startling Caleb as much as he'd startled her.

He was wearing nothing but a baby blanket around his waist, tied in a knot, Roman-style.

Swiftly, she turned her back on him and covered her eyes.

"Sorry!" they both said at once.

"No, I'm sorry. I thought you were in the boys' nursery," Caleb said.

"It's okay," April said on a rush. "Of course, you need to take a shower to wash that stuff off you. I wasn't thinking. I'll just squeeze past you, and—" She backed up, determined to get past him without seeing more than she had. Instead, she bumped into him, and he put a hand out to steady her.

"I'm okay!" She darted around him, reaching out

to grab the doorknob and pull the door shut behind her. Pulse racing, she leaned against the wall, relaxing only when she heard the shower turn on. "Oh, boy," she said under her breath. "Now I know why women throw themselves at him like grenades set to explode on impact."

Great-looking in clothes, he was even better nude. With a baby blanket around his waist, he was awesome.

She'd made love with him. And though she hadn't been able to see much on their wedding night since neither of them had stopped what they were doing to flip on a light, she knew what that pink-and-blue-giraffes-print blanket was hiding.

A groan escaped her, and this time it wasn't because his confidence annoyed her. It was because she remembered—and because he was right about sneak attacks.

She wanted to be in his arms again, making love—and she shouldn't have in the first place. There was no reason to make love with a man with whom she wasn't in love. Wasn't going to marry.

"Not marry for real," she qualified to herself.

"Got any towels?" Caleb asked, jerking the door open and peering through the crack.

She barely stopped the scream that nearly tore from her throat. His hair was wet, his chest glistening from the shower. She didn't dare let her gaze wander any lower, instead remaining steadfast on his face. "Under the sink," she said quickly.

"Thanks." He gave her a devilish smile, and slowly closed the door.

Darn it! He knows exactly what he's doing to me—and he's loving it.

By NIGHTFALL, they were both exhausted.

"I knew it was going to be a lot of work. I just didn't know how much," Caleb said. "It's a good thing you've got me here."

She had moved an extra chair into the den area so that they wouldn't both have to sit on the sofa. Her chair was plush and comfy, and she'd curled her feet up under her, relaxing into the softness. "Having all these children will probably make me very ready to see you whenever you're going to be around," she said, her voice already sleepy.

Did he ever have a surprise for her, little-miss-I've-got-to-do-everything-myself. "I've taken indefinite leave from my job as well. I plan to be here until things get a bit more manageable."

Her eyes snapped open, and he couldn't tell if she was pleasantly or unpleasantly shocked. "Why?"

He shrugged, trying to act casual. It was her house, after all. He was the interloper, even though they'd planned for him to stay here once the babies arrived. But he was pretty certain April had been thinking more of a nighttime schedule for him rather than around-the-clock. His feeling was that the tiny lady might need more help than she thought, and he didn't even want to envision a scenario where she might get herself in a jam with no one here to help her. "I want to put all my efforts into finding Jenny, for one thing. It's tough to do that, and work a full-time job. I had a lot of leave built up, since I don't like to take vacations."

Hell, he'd never had any reason to. Where would he have gone? Staying busy kept him from remembering and thinking about things he didn't want to. He hadn't even really had to ask for an indefinite leave because he had so much paid time coming to him. "I plan to do nothing but help you take care of the babies, and find Jenny." *And make certain you don't overwork yourself and make yourself ill. That wouldn't do anyone any good, and it would worry me real bad.*

But he didn't make the pronouncement out loud because it would bring Independence Day with all the stars and stripes and marching-band protesting forth from April.

"Are you sure? I hate for you to have to give up your life because of me, Caleb. What about your dad? Doesn't that make an awful lot of work—"

Caleb held up a hand. "It's fine, April. You ought to know by now that Dad would rather have me here so he can get hour-by-hour reports. In fact, it's probably either me or Dad."

She smiled a little, her eyes sparkling. "You're probably right about your dad."

He intended to be right about a lot of things.

Mainly, that he thought it was best if he was here with her.

"But I'm not used to living with a man around the clock," she said worriedly. "There's only one bathroom. The hall is narrow. The kitchen is small. I never did buy a futon."

"April, I'm pretty adaptable. You're not announcing a headline by telling me this is a dollhouse. It's just right for you, and I like it because of that. I would have been fairly weirded out to find out that you lived in a house with massive leather furniture and an animal's skull and horns on the wall."

She giggled. "You'll have to settle for needle-point flowers."

"I find it rather peaceful," he fibbed. He hadn't looked closely at the walls of her house. Mainly he looked at her.

"Maybe we'd better set some ground rules," she suggested.

"Okay. I'll take the babies at night. That will leave me free during the day to talk to people about Jenny. And I'll never, ever, walk out of the bathroom nude. What do you think about that set of ground rules? You don't have to make the same agreement, of course," he said smoothly.

April considered his suggestion. She felt her skin blush, and by the raising of Caleb's eyebrow, she knew he was fully aware that she'd been mulling over the last part of his idea rather than the baby arrangements.

"I never walk around nude, which may disappoint you," she said, making her voice stern. "Did you walk around in the buff in your apartment?"

"Not much," he admitted. "I only put blinds up in my bedroom. Didn't spend much time in my apartment, actually. Too quiet."

"Well, it won't be quiet here." April got up, hearing a baby squawk come over the monitor. She crept down the hall to check on the babies, but the squeak she'd heard was only Matthew letting out a tiny wail before going back to sleep.

"You'll like me being gone during the day," he said softly when she returned. "It's the best way, April, because you'll be asleep when I'm doing duty with the babies. I know you're not going to be one hundred percent comfortable with me in your space."

She shook her head. "I guess I won't. I wouldn't with anyone, most likely."

"It's hard when you've been on your own to suddenly share living quarters. I'm going to try to keep my intrusiveness to a minimum."

I'm not certain that's exactly what I want, she thought. "I'd rather have you here than anyone else, though."

"You would?"

He seemed so astonished that she felt sorry for him. "I'm sorry, Caleb. I haven't meant to make you feel unwelcome. I'm simply so focused on learning to be a mom that I haven't taken the time to say thank you. But I do appreciate everything you've done. None of this would have been possible without you.'' *That* she meant from the bottom of her heart.

He was so quiet. His stillness told her that her words had touched him. She'd have to file that away for the future: *Caleb really likes to know his heroic efforts are truly appreciated.* She wasn't used to that sort of give-and-take since she hadn't had many relationships. She didn't like to count on anyone, or for a man to try to take care of her. Somehow, Caleb was doing it without setting off the old alarms she normally felt.

Maybe it's because I know it's not forever. And yet, she liked knowing she'd made him happy with her sincere gratitude.

And then it hit her. Caleb liked to know his heroic efforts were appreciated—because he felt as if he'd failed the only other person he'd let really close to him.

So that was the cementing ingredient in this arrangement. She had never wanted anyone to take care of her. He needed to take care of her because he'd let his partner down, in his mind.

Caleb was trying very hard, with teasing and sensual innuendo, not to let her become aware that he was trying to take care of her and the children. But it had turned into a mission for him, much as it had for Jackson. She and the babies filled a gap for them, healed something Caleb needed healed.

She was a nurse. There was no way she couldn't respond to his desire to heal.

He had given up a lot to help her with what she most wanted.

She could make a supreme effort not to mind his care and protection. He wasn't trying to take her independence; he wasn't wanting her to become dependent upon him, as some men did. She didn't have to be afraid that he'd desert her, because they both knew this marriage was nonpermanent.

It was a small thing to do for a man who needed something she could provide so easily. What it would do to her heart, she wasn't certain, but then, her heart wasn't the only one on the line.

AFTER ONE LAST RUSH of feeding, diapering and comforting with the babies, April finally decided she'd easily take Caleb up on his offer of nighttime assistance. "Good night," she told him. "Please make yourself at home in any way, Caleb. I mean that."

"Thanks," he said sincerely. "You get some rest."

Her eyes communicated uncertain tension. Beneath all the teasing he peppered her with was a desire to ignore how much he wanted her. Caleb had never wanted anything so bad in his life. Making love to her, feeling her underneath him, being inside her—all of that felt as if he'd been welcomed home.

But he knew their lovemaking was a one-night

happening. April wasn't cut out for a short-term affair, and he didn't regard her in that light. But it was enough to be here with her now, the closest thing to a family of his own he might ever know. Husband, wife, children.

But the tension he saw in her eyes, *that* he could erase. "Go to bed," he said softly. "I've got it all under control."

"Okay. Thank you." She backed away, still hesitant, before turning down the short hall and disappearing into her room.

"And that's that," he said to himself. "Newly-wed night number one. No problem. Under control, tight lid, cool temps." He flipped a few channels on the television, keeping a tight ear on the monitor for the babies over the next hour. The late-night comedians weren't that funny, the classic sports channel had lost its appeal and a romantic movie wasn't what he needed tonight, of all nights. Not when he couldn't be diverted from thinking about April, tucked in her white bed.

Kicking his feet up on the sofa, he let the cushy softness surround him, forced everything from his mind and fell asleep.

A WARY SENSATION hit him early in the a.m. He'd only dozed, he was pretty certain, listening with one ear to the monitor, and his consciousness unscrambling what he'd learned about Jenny in his mind.

Something he couldn't put his finger on had

awakened him. His eyes snapped open in the darkness, adjusting to the flickering light of the television. Warm fingers rested lightly against his neck; a bare arm trailed over his shoulder.

April sat on the floor, her forehead against the sofa seat cushion. She slept in a sideways kneeling position that had to be uncomfortable. He registered that she was touching him in a manner which was clearly nonsexual. Comforting.

He sighed, realizing he must have shouted in his sleep again. She'd mentioned it before, and the only reason he didn't realize he did it so often was because there was no one around his apartment to complain about it.

Or comfort him.

Hopefully he hadn't awakened the babies when he'd yelled. Slowly, he pulled to a sitting position, then gathered April into his arms as if she were a child. *Well, definitely not a child,* he thought as her curves melted against him, accepting his action. More like a very delicate, very delicious woman.

It appeared he was going to keep her up every night with his nightmares; she was going to keep him up every night with a serious case of unquenchable desire.

Eventually, they'd have to find a way to sleep, or they'd be no good for the babies. Slipping her into her bed, Caleb stared down at April.

What the hell. He pulled off his shoes, kept everything else on and got in the bed, scooting up against her back. She sighed in her sleep and reached to pull his arm over her waist.

Promising, Caleb decided as he closed his eyes. *A little scary, but promising.*

Chapter Fourteen

Sneak attack. Caleb had clearly pulled one on her. He was in her bed, lying spoon-style up against her back, snoring quietly in her ear.

Far different from what he'd been doing in the early a.m. The shrieks of agony had pulled her from her bed in a fright as she rushed to the sofa. A hand on his forehead and quiet murmurs had chased away whatever was torturing his mind's eye, yet still she'd been unable to leave him for fear the nightmare would recur. It ripped her soul to hear such a strong man cry out, calling for back-up.

Shuddering, she knew that whatever he'd seen was locked in his mind forever, lying in wait to feed on his unguarded moments. She could not allow the man she'd married—for however long—to suffer in such a way. Not when he'd done so much good for her, easing her suffering. For better, for worse, in sickness, and in health.

She'd kneeled beside the sofa and stroked his head. He'd never wakened again—until he'd carried her to bed. Obviously, he'd decided that sleeping with her in the bed was preferable to both of them being uncomfortable on the sofa, and a mature reflection of their situation made her agree.

Of course, it was the simple symbol of the bed which alarmed her. A bed was intimate with two people in it, inviting closeness and a feeling of bonding that worried her.

Jenny would come back, as she should. And Caleb would leave.

Was it wrong for her to guard against feeling more for him, when she already realized she felt far too much as it was?

A weak cry came over the monitor Caleb had parked beside the bed. She snapped it off before he could wake, slid from the bed and changed into sweatpants and a top. Closing the bedroom door, she left her husband sleeping in her bed.

The truth was, she really liked seeing his broad form in her pristine, delicate room. The dolls had kept her from being lonely and scared before, but nothing had ever felt as good to her as waking to find Caleb's strong warmth against her, a strange shelter from everything she'd wanted to chase away, and never could.

"WHY DIDN'T YOU wake me up?" Caleb asked.

"You needed your sleep." April shot him a look, taking in his hair, sexily awry, his jeans rumpled and somewhat loose.

"So did you. Apparently, you didn't get much."

Turning away so she wouldn't think too much about how handsome he was, April fussed with a baby diaper. "I feel very refreshed, actually."

Silence met that. Apparently, he didn't want to bring up them sleeping in the same bed, or the nightmares, any more than she did.

"I did some thinking last night," he said suddenly.

"Oh?"

"Despite the missing person's report, and the police looking for Jenny, no one has come forward to say that they've seen her in a little over a month. If she were in the area, she would have seen the news reports on television, read in the newspaper about her babies going home. She's not in the area."

A sick shiver slid along April's spine. She laid Craig in his crib and went to tend Matthew. "What's next then, if that's what you've come to believe?"

"It occurred to me last night that anyone I talked to hasn't had the knowledge of Jenny's past that you do."

She glanced up at him, her mouth open. "No, Caleb, I am not holding back anything I know about Jenny just so that I can keep her children."

"I didn't say you were," he said, his tone soft.

April drew up sharp. "Please don't play mind games with me. I didn't like it when you theorized that I might have projected my needs onto Jenny, filling in the realization of the mother she needed for her children. And I don't like you overtly suggesting that I might be harboring information about her."

"April. Relax, babe."

His soothing tone did take some of the steel out of her spine. She went back to fixing Matthew's diaper. "I want Jenny to come back."

Silence met her statement, and that unnerved her. "I do, Caleb," she insisted. "I believe that children belong with their parents whenever possible, whenever it's best for that to happen."

"I know you do."

"I won't tell you that having these babies in my care and in my home hasn't opened up a longing for children of my own. A true family of my very own. It's intense, and it's a deeper wish than it's ever been before. But I can have my own children, Caleb. In fact, I dream of it. I've always wanted children, and so, one day. One day."

He was silent, so she peered his way again. The look on his face startled her. "What's wrong? What did I say?"

"I don't want children," he said slowly.

She frowned at him. "What are these?" she asked, pointing to the children.

"Mine for the time being. Little people who need a good start in the world, that I am capable of providing. But I don't want any of my own."

His stark reaction puzzled her. "I don't know what you're getting at."

"I don't know, either." He swept her with a gaze that seemed longing, and yet, somehow, unhappy. "I'm sorry. I don't know why I said that. It was just a...gut reaction."

He *had* surprised her, and somehow she was disappointed that he wouldn't want children of his own, but the topic was too personal to discuss with him. "Were we talking about something else before we got sidetracked?" Picking up Matthew, she held him close. "Something about Jenny?"

His hand went up in surrender. "Without you thinking that I'm accusing you of anything—"

"Well, you did before, and it was an unpleasant leap you made."

"Okay. I apologize. It's in my nature to—"

"Run through the trails of someone's mind. I know. Jenny talked to me a lot, but I've told you everything I know, and I'm not hiding anything."

"Okay. Slow down a minute. Listen to me. I want you to think about your childhood."

She creased her lips together. "I won't think about it for long, so hurry up with what you want to know."

"Hold Matthew, close your eyes and listen to my voice. Jenny's childhood was somewhat similar to yours. You had that in common. You grew up in what state?"

"Texas."

"Did you have that in common?"

Her eyes opened. "Ohio. Jenny was from a small

town in Ohio, David had once lived on a farm in Texas. They had some kind of tree in common. Um, pecan. I think.''

He nodded at her, and April's stomach seemed to reverse inside her. "I didn't withhold that from you. And it could mean nothing.''

"It could mean nothing, and no, you did not keep that information from me. Idle conversations of no seeming importance take place all the time. But hopefully, with any luck, that may be a salient piece of something I can go on.''

"How could Jenny have gotten to Ohio?'' Panic began to rise inside her. "She was sick, she had no money. It was Christmastime.''

He nodded. "And those may be many of the reasons why she could have gone back to a place where she had something in common with the man she loved—and lost.''

CALEB DIDN'T KNOW why he hadn't thought of it before, but somehow sitting in front of the television watching everything and anything had brought the question to the fore of his mind: Why would Jenny not come to her children after seeing them on the news at night? He knew she'd had no intention of coming back, but there was only one reason she wouldn't have sent some kind of message to April once she knew that the children had gone home healthy from the hospital: She wasn't anywhere where she could see the local news.

"I'll be back tonight. Count on a good night's sleep," he told April, shrugging on a black cloth jacket with a warm lining. First, the truck stop on the highway out of town. He'd already checked the bus stops once in the beginning of his investigation; no names had matched Jenny's or any variation thereof.

But the truck stop—until April had said Ohio, Caleb hadn't had an idea of how far the quads' mother might have intended to go. There was lots of goodwill at Christmastime, and truckers were a notoriously helpful lot. It wouldn't have been all that hard for Jenny to have found a softie to give her a ride "home for the holidays."

And a desperate young girl wouldn't think twice about telling such a tale if she meant to return to the last place that might hold happy memories for her. Anyplace but where she'd lost her husband.

He was the champion at trying to outrun memories. It wasn't all that hard to understand Jenny's motivation.

Milling around the truck stop for thirty minutes asking questions, he came upon an older lady named Rosemarie who worked there. Yes, she'd seen a young girl about a month or so ago, and the only reason that stuck out in her mind was because the girl seemed weak and somehow disoriented. At Christmas, she was concerned that the teenager was a runaway. The girl, whose name was April, said she'd just delivered a stillbirth and her husband had left her.

Her tale had elicited sympathy and a hot meal from her, as well as a ride from her sister, who was a trucker.

To Cleveland, Ohio. But from there, the girl meant to go to some small town in Ohio, where her family had once lived.

Sharp instinct twisted Caleb's gut. Jenny didn't want to be found, but he had to find her, for everyone's sake. She needed help, and grief counseling. The babies needed their mother, and she needed them. April needed Jenny to return, not the least of the reasons was that she could never truly adopt the children without Jenny's legal approval. As April's was a temporary foster home, the babies could be removed at any time and assigned to different homes. Caleb needed Jenny to return before he fell any farther into the pretend marriage he'd suggested. Because he was seriously in danger of that—and when April had mentioned wanting her own children this morning, he'd known that there was no future in their marriage at all.

He would do anything on this planet, anything at all: run into gunfire to try to save a buddy, protect the innocent, serve the public, be a father to four abandoned children.

But he would not get a woman pregnant with his child. And most definitely not April. Delicate, gentle, sweetly caring April.

Never.

JACKSON CALLED that morning before he stopped by, ostensibly bringing baby blankets in case she didn't have enough.

"It's going to be cold outside," he said gruffly.

But April could tell by the hungry look in his eyes that he was starved to hold the babies. And she was glad of the company. It gave her a fast break and a chance to eat some lunch. "I'm glad you stopped by, Jackson. These babies have kept me busy. They may be having trouble getting used to the new environment. Although it's quieter here, they may have gotten used to the constant lights and voices and sounds in the hospital. They just can't seem to settle today."

She knew them well enough from taking care of them in the hospital to know that they were out of sorts. Of course, the second that Jackson picked up Melissa and balanced her in his arms, she quieted.

"I think she feels the resonance of your voice."

"Anything this tiny thinks my deep voice sounds like a bass drum. But I'll talk quietly," he said to Melissa.

The baby's eyelids drooped. Jackson seemed delighted that he had comforted the baby as he settled onto the sofa. "The night was uneventful?"

April felt a blush sweep her. She knew he was asking about the babies, but the night had been uneventful for *her*. As every night would be. "Yes.

They slept most of the night, then only required one feeding.''

"How are you and Caleb working the schedule?''

"He's nights, I'm days. But I'm not expecting the babies to sleep all of another night. I think it had to have been a result of all the excitement of moving locations, and they were extra tired. I'm paying for it today.''

"I could come over every day for a feeding time so that you can nap,'' he said eagerly. "I don't do much for lunch at the office, and until they're more settled, I'd be happy to do it. Bri offered to do the same, one or two days a week. We could switch out.''

April smiled to herself as she made a sandwich in the kitchen. The McCallum generosity was more than she'd ever expected. It was what being a family was all about—and as much as she loved her adoptive mother and father, the McCallums were a bonus. As were the babies.

I almost wish it would never end. I wish it wasn't a watercolor dream-come-true that might wash away any minute.

It wasn't just her dream; it was Jackson's, too. "Don't you and Bri have enough to do where babies are concerned?''

"I figure this crew's not permanently ours. And they may need us more. Bri's got a real husband for her, and a real father for her children. She also has a housekeeper. You're mostly on your own, and I admire that greatly, but I don't think it should mean you have to do it all on your own.''

"Thank you, Jackson.'' She came to sit in the den, watching him drink up the babies in their four rolling bassinets crowded throughout the small room.

"Well, you're a daughter to me. You're married to my son, and that makes you family.''

Jackson didn't look up, and April paused in the act of putting the sandwich in her mouth. He knew that the marriage was bogus, contingent upon the situation with the infants. But he'd sounded so serious. As if he wanted to believe her marriage to Caleb would become forever.

"Where is Caleb?''

April shrugged. "Trying to follow leads for Jenny.''

"You know he'll find her. Eventually.''

She waited, wondering what Jackson was trying to tell her.

"There's no one like Caleb,'' he said heavily, "when it comes to thinking through a case. He's got a special talent, and he was a damn fine officer.''

"He says he'll never go back,'' April said. "He says that part of his life is over.''

"That's true. I don't always agree with it, but now that I see these children, I think it's best if he didn't.''

"It's not forever, Jackson,'' she said gently.

"I know.'' He laid Melissa in her bassinet, stroking her back before covering her with a blanket. "I just want you to be prepared for the fact that Caleb will find Jenny. It's his job, and he won't quit until he does. And I think you should be prepared for whatever happens when Jenny returns."

"I think it's best that she does. As soon as possible. Children need their mother, if at all possible and appropriate."

"I agree. But take it from me, April," he said, his voice distant and emotional, "what's best isn't always what happens."

Chapter Fifteen

Caleb drove his car, not really certain how to tell April that he had a strong lead now on where to find Jenny. Technically, he should probably tell the appropriate law enforcement agency. The thing was, the fact that Jenny had gone out of state pretty much left local authorities without much jurisdiction, even if they felt like pursuing his flimsy information.

But what really nagged at him was the truck-stop lady's words about Jenny. He'd gotten the feeling that Jenny had been so tired and so desperate that folks had taken pity on her. He really didn't think unfamiliar police officers tracking her would do anything to alleviate the upset the girl was already under.

Though she didn't know Caleb, either, the fact that she'd used April's name while traveling gave him hope that she might see in him a comforting presence. He was helping to care for her children—surely those two combined facts would tame Jenny's fears.

Taming April's would be another. Envisioning going home with his news that someone had, in fact, seen Jenny and helped her leave the state, he felt April's first reaction would be relief. And then concern for Jenny.

Whether she would admit it or not, some trepidation would be mixed in there as well. In her mind, April knew these children weren't hers forever. She had already decided to have a child of her own when the inevitable day of reuniting Jenny with her family arrived. He'd seen her decision and the desire in her eyes.

But she hadn't looked at him as if he'd had the answer to the other side of the parenting dilemma—and he'd let her know in no uncertain terms that he was not a father candidate.

That left him with an uncomfortable, gnawing feeling in his stomach. His mother had died in childbirth after delivering him. April wanted children of her own; he would not jeopardize her health. That meant that no matter how much he knew himself to be falling for her, she would never be his. Not his wife, and not the mother of his children.

It meant he had to find Jenny fast, and get the hell out of April's house. This convenient marriage needed to come to a swift, merciful conclusion.

He was in serious danger of losing his heart. Maybe he'd already lost it—a terrified voice inside him was warning that he was ever more deeply involved in a matter outside his control.

Going inside the small dollhouse of a home, he saw the wreckage of the day by the dim lamp April had left on. Blankets and burp cloths lay over bassinets; empty bottles littered the coffee table. He smiled, seeing at once that April's day had been busy.

He felt pretty certain that she'd loved every minute of it.

Laying his keys on the kitchen counter, he began putting away the bottles in the sink, washing them out for the next day. The scattered burp cloths he tossed in a washer filled with hot water; he checked the nighttime supply of premade bottles in the fridge. Everything looked good to go, and since he was the nightshift, he decided to go down the hall and swipe the monitor out of April's room. He should have called her; should have checked on her; should have told her when he'd be home.

But that would have smacked of a real marriage. He wasn't ready for *Honey, I'm on my way home.* Not now. Not when he knew what he had to do.

Before he could open April's bedroom door, his cell phone rang. Swiftly, he pulled it from his pocket. "Hello?" he asked quietly, moving back toward the den.

"Caleb?"

He frowned. "Yes?"

"This is the lady you spoke with at the truck stop. Rosemarie."

"Yeah. Right. I remember." He'd given her his

number in case she thought of any further details after he left. Many times people did, once they had a chance to think things through without him standing around. And sometimes they just needed enough time to think through airing their conscience—and to give him a call.

"I just needed some time to think about what you wanted to know about. The girl," she said uncertainly.

"That's all right, Rosemarie."

"I didn't tell you everything. I needed to think about what the right thing to do was. I mean, that gal was so frightened. And I didn't know her, but I sure did feel sorry for her."

"I know. She needs help and understanding right now."

"Well, it was Christmas and…anyway, she's at my mother's in Pecan Grove," Rosemarie said on a rush. "My sister took her there so she'd be safe until we could find her family, or until she got well enough to do whatever she needed to do. I can give you the address," Rosemarie told him, her voice soft, "but my mom's grown real fond of her. She's good company. All I ask is that…is that you be gentle with her. She's too young to be as sad as she is."

"It's okay, Rosemarie," Caleb said, his voice soothing. "I appreciate all you've done for her. I'll go and get her, and I promise you, I'll keep in touch with you and let you know that she's getting along fine. She's been through a lot, but she's got people here who are going to help her."

"You looked like a kind man. You looked like you honestly cared about what happened to her. I wouldn't have called you if I hadn't thought so."

Conscience attack. He admired Rosemarie for choosing to call him. She clearly wanted to protect Jenny. "You've done the right thing, Rosemarie. I'll be in touch."

Shutting off the cell phone, he scribbled the address she'd given him on a piece of paper in the kitchen. He called the airport and scheduled a flight into the nearest big city around Pecan Grove for tomorrow, early a.m.

Then he went down the hall, slowly opening April's door to grab the monitor. She was clearly exhausted, one leg thrown out of the sheets, her arm over her eyes. The light from the hallway showed him that she was wearing a cozy flannel gown. Nothing sexy about that—and yet, there was. He just thought everything about April was delicate and feminine.

He so wanted to take care of her. He so wanted to shield her from all the bad hurts in the world.

The cop instinct to protect had to be turned back. She had warned him that men wanted to take care of her, and that she did not welcome that.

But he was going to get the biological mother of the children whom she loved. With one simple plane flight, he would irreversibly change the course of their marriage. Once Jenny realized how much support she had in helping to raise these children, she would want her family back together.

April and he would have no reason to continue their marriage. Social Services would no longer impact their lives.

Tonight would be the last chance to touch April, to hold her, and to feel her shallow breathing in the deepest part of his body. It was wrong, maybe it was taking from her something she wasn't willing to give, it might even be unchivalrous as hell, but just for tonight he wanted to sleep up against her again.

He could sincerely apologize in the morning. Or tomorrow night, when he came home with Jenny. It really wouldn't make any difference, because everything between them would be finished.

He'd return April's key, and pretty much walk out of her life to sleep in his own bed. His barely furnished apartment with the blinds only in the bedroom because he wasn't there enough to bother with them anywhere else.

Something that felt unnaturally like dread filled him. He didn't hesitate any longer, but pulled off his boots. Same as he had last night, he slid into the bed fully clothed.

Same as she had last night, April reached for his arm, pulling his cold, windswept body up against her back, so that his knees securely pulled up under her flannel-covered body and his arm over her waist to hold her.

At that precise moment, Caleb knew he was forever lost to the petite nurse. The wife he couldn't keep.

WHEN APRIL AWAKENED the next morning to the cries of babies going full tilt, she knew she'd slept hard. At some point in the night, she'd relaxed into the deepest sleep she'd experienced in some time. The babies hadn't cried, or if they had, she'd slept right through it, knowing that Caleb was on duty. She'd heard no yells from him, either, so he'd slept soundly as well.

The only evidence he'd been in the house were the clean bottles and dried, folded blankets and burp cloths. And yet, she remembered being held in the night.

Think I've found Jenny. Gone to check, was the note he'd left written on the table. Holding Matthew against her, April felt her stomach pitch at the words, just a little. Hope that Jenny would be found and reunited with her children. Fear for Jenny's condition. Some regret that the babies might not be in her care much longer.

All of these emotions smote her at once. It was almost too much. With tears stinging her eyes, she brought all the babies into the den, changing their diapers and then beginning the juggling act of feeding them.

The doorbell rang and her heart jumped in her chest. "Who is it?"

"Bri."

"Oh, good. Help is on the way, you guys." Still holding the baby she was feeding, April got up and opened the door. "Please excuse my nightgown. I have never been so glad to see you."

Bri laughed. "Did Dad tell you I was planning to stop by?"

"He made some vague reference about the two of you plotting a schedule to assist me. Grab a bottle and help yourself."

Bri did just that, shrugging out of her coat and scooping up Chloe, whose racket seemed the most intense at that moment. "So, how's it going?" She swept a glance around the room. "It looks very successful, I must say. If I didn't know better, I'd think you were handling everything with your customary aplomb. Are you?"

"I don't know. Some things, yes. Other things, no."

"Well, let's start with the things you're not handling as well." Bri gave her a mischievous grin. "Those are the most fun, usually."

"I don't know how to tell you this," April said carefully, "but I think I'm crazy about your brother."

"Oh. Bad thing to be crazy about your husband," she teased.

With a stab of conscience, April remembered that

Bri thought the marriage was a love-at-first-sight match. "Well, I mean that I...I don't know." She sighed, wishing she could tell Bri more. They hadn't had much reserve with each other in the past—and yet, there was no one else she could confide in. "Caleb left a note this morning that said he thought he knew where Jenny was."

"Really? That's awesome! Dad said Caleb would find her, and Daddy really does know best in this instance."

"Yes." April lowered her gaze for just a moment. "Bri, Caleb and I got married so that we could get temporary custody of the babies."

Bri stared at her. "The pieces are beginning to fit. I'm sure I suspected, but decided I would over-look it in the hopes that you two might decide mar-riage was too good to pass up. Not many women would want to throw my brother back into the dating pond. I mean, he can be annoying—he is my brother after all—but I'm not blind to how women feel about him. I just wouldn't want you to leave our family, so I was hoping his charm would affect you the same way."

It did. His charm and so much more than surface effects had caught at April's heart. Unfortunately, she was keeping a secret, one that she knew wasn't going to be pleasant for Caleb.

"So, basically what you're trying to tell me is that since Caleb's gone to get Jenny, most likely any reason you two had to stay married is about to be null and void.''

''In a nutshell, that's it.''

''I see. Well, that stinks,'' Bri said, shifting the baby to her other arm and adjusting the bottle. ''But you said you think you're crazy about him.''

''Yes. I fear I am.''

Her smile was teasing, and yet sympathetic. ''Dad has the notion that Caleb really likes you, April.''

''I think we…have a mutual attraction. Still, some things are off-limits for both of us.''

''Oh, I see,'' Bri said, her tone changing to one of awareness.

''No, no. It doesn't have to do with what you're thinking.'' April frowned for a second, realizing that her problem did have to do with sex, though Bri obviously thought she'd meant their problem had something to do with the bedroom, which it most definitely didn't—or that they hadn't made love, which they most definitely had.

''I'm late,'' she said suddenly, needing to get it out of her system, no matter what happened once her worry was voiced.

''Where are you going?'' Bri asked, sitting up to glance at the clock.

''My period is late,'' April said, slowly enunciating the words so Bri would understand.

Bri sank back into the sofa, cradling the baby in her arms. ''You are?''

''Yes. I was approximately three-quarters through

my cycle when we married. Since I've always been regular as clockwork, I thought it was a safe time. But with all the stress about the babies, and Jenny, and Matthew being...rolled into another part of the hospital for a while, my schedule might have been off."

Bri's eyes were wide. "And you think you might be expecting."

"I don't know. I've never been late before. Never."

Bri stared at her, her expression stricken. "Well, there's no point in jumping the gun before you know for certain. You should get a home pregnancy test next week, or make an appointment at Maitland. I can arrange to be here with the children if you decide to go see an OB-GYN."

"I might have you do that," April said miserably. "You know, I've always wanted to have a child of my own, but this is not going to be good news."

"You know, then? That Caleb isn't going to take it very well if you are?"

She nodded, hearing the sympathy in Bri's voice. "I know. He's always been clear about the fact that he doesn't want children of his own. And that's what worries me so much."

"So let me think this through for a minute." Bri got up to put the baby in the bassinet, reaching for the last infant who was quite ready for breakfast. "My brother has gone to get Jenny. You're both expecting Jenny to want to come home to her chil-

dren, once she sees them again, and once she real-
izes she has a larger support system than she knew.''

''I think so. That's the way it seemed.''

''And so then, you and Caleb can quietly divorce
because you were only together for the sake of the
children. Only now you think you might be pregnant, which, while it won't make Caleb happy, he
would never dream of going through with a divorce
then.''

April nodded.

''And you didn't want him that way.''

April shook her head.

''You got married because of someone else's
babies, but you worry he won't want you if you're
expecting his baby.'' Bri bobbed her head. ''It's
convoluted, but it's Caleb. But you could be bor-
rowing trouble. In a few days, you might start.''

''It's true.'' She hoped so.

''Wait a little longer before you worry too much.
Work through the Jenny aspect of your marriage,
and once the babies are reunited with their mother,
I'll be curious to see if my brother is as easy to get
rid of as you seem to think he will be. By then, a
home pregnancy test will show something, and
you'll know whether you have anything to tell him
or not. But since there's really not a good sure way
to know until then, just wait a couple more days. At
least, that's my take on it.''

''All right.'' But she couldn't help worrying
somewhat.

"From a medical point of view, I can't help wondering if you're late because you're tired. The month has been stressful. You don't really want to give up these children, though you know it's for the best if Jenny is in any way able emotionally to handle parenting them. It's a lot, April. And you've shouldered a lot of it alone."

"Actually, Caleb is very supportive. I couldn't have asked for more."

"Well, then," Bri said softly, "don't give up on him so soon. He's a bit of a chicken when it comes to certain things he doesn't want to face, but so are we all. You happen to be accidentally picking at his biggest bogey of all, but…"

"But what?" April demanded, not comforted at all.

"I don't know. Will it help if I tell you I'll pound my brother if he doesn't take it like a man if the two of you are expecting?"

April laughed shakily. "It helps that you say it, but the actual action wouldn't do me much good. I'm a healer by nature, and couldn't bear to see you hurt him."

"Well, then don't you hurt him, either," Bri told her in a gentle voice. "If Dad says Caleb really cares for you, April, then I suggest we give Caleb a chance to find that out for himself."

Chapter Sixteen

"I actually like the idea that I could be an aunt in nine months," Bri said, her face turning impish with delight.

"Don't even say that out loud!" April cautioned. "Let's not put it in the air where it might hang and somehow become fact."

"Like a speech balloon in a comic strip."

"I suppose, except that there is nothing funny about this." April carried some diapers into the laundry room and came back. "I know that I have what it takes to be a good mother. What concerns me, though, is do I have what it takes to be a good wife?"

"Why would you think you don't?"

April shook her head. "Inability to willingly form attachments, maybe?"

"You said you think you're falling for my brother," Bri pointed out. "He might be falling for you. Without an unexpected fly in the ointment, matters might proceed in a surprisingly romantic fashion.''

"You don't think that me being pregnant wouldn't be a fly?''

"Well, is he kind to you?''

"Caleb's kind to everyone.''

"Yes, but does he hold you at all? Kiss you?''

The question brought a sudden blush to April's face. "He kissed me the night we got married.''

"Obviously,'' Bri said, her tone dry. "But other than that?''

"No,'' April admitted. "We probably both tacitly agreed that the one night was somehow a reaction to all the champagne and good wishes flowing our way.''

"Or a reaction to secret wishes in your souls. Caleb's a pussycat, April, though he rarely allows anyone to know it.''

"He sleeps against me in the night,'' April said softly, "when he thinks I don't realize he's doing it.''

"I don't get it. Details.''

She took a deep breath. "When I'm in bed, for the past two nights I've awakened to either find him in my bed, or some clue that he was there. And then I remember that I felt him against my back, kind of snuggling me.''

"Oh, that's sweet,'' Bri breathed. "Almost like he wants to give you affection and to receive it but is too worried about making things uncomfortable between you to ask for it."

"Maybe," April said doubtfully. "I would never ask him why he does it. The truth is, I like it, hard as it is to admit. So I don't mention it, because I don't want him to stop."

"Oh, April. You guys have got so much airing out to do in so little time. The biggest part of all of this is that you've had to compress so much into so little time. I know you'll miss them, but if Jenny's coming home, and the babies and her start a family, it may be the very best thing for your marriage. I always have faith that illusion is some parts real. Isn't that the basis of fairy tales?"

April didn't answer. Fairy tales were a matter reserved for children who didn't grow up in orphanages—or at least not for her. Reality had always been her companion, and the main reason she depended upon herself.

Caleb sleeping with her was comforting, but the reality was, their marriage was an illusion.

AFTER THE BABIES were settled into their bassinets for their naps, and Bri left, April picked up the mess left from the morning round of feeding and diapering. Then she decided that a homecoming—if Caleb did bring Jenny home—called for a celebration.

She decided to bake a cake. The fragrance of warm chocolate cake alone would be soothing. Mixing the ingredients was a comforting process, giving her something to concentrate on other than whether her marriage would essentially end tonight or not.

But when she got to the canned frosting, it seemed that there was nothing left to focus on. Jenny belonged with her children, and Caleb and April had done the right thing. Not a forever thing, but a right thing.

Bri was right: So much had been compressed into such a short time that April almost felt as if *she'd* been the one to give birth to the quads. And the quads had birthed her marriage. She was going to miss them, and she was going to miss Caleb.

Tears filled her eyes. Sinking onto the wooden stool, she popped the top on the canned chocolate frosting and ate a big spoonful right out of the can. And then she let the tears fall because the frosting splurge wasn't going to make her feel any better.

It tasted good, but it wasn't sugar-and-spice-and-everything-nice like the babies were. And it wasn't snips-and-snails-and-puppy-dog-tails like her big strong husband.

IN THE END, April managed to get more frosting on the cake than in her mouth.

She was actually fairly pleased with her efforts. Little yellow frosting flowers adorned the top edge of the cake. Squeezing those out of the frosting gun had only taken a little while longer, and it made the cake look pretty.

She took a shower, checked on the babies and fell asleep on the sofa for a nap.

Fifteen minutes later, by her watch, all four babies wanted attention again. "You didn't sleep very long," she cooed, wondering if they sensed her unsettled state. "I wonder if your formula is the wrong kind."

Checking in diapers, she decided that the babies had simply returned to their routine in the hospital where there'd been a lot of noise and action. Or at least more than there was in her tiny home. "Maybe it got too quiet and startled you," she said. "When it gets warmer in the spring, I'm going to put all of you in a stroller and walk you every chance I get."

She could do that even if the babies weren't living in her house. Brightening, she realized that Jenny would still need help. *Her* help. She wouldn't be separated from them the way her mind was envisioning.

The front door opened, and to April's astonishment, Jenny walked in, followed by Caleb.

"Jenny!" Leaping to her feet, April rushed to hug the girl. Over Jenny's shoulder, she could see Caleb looking at her, his face concerned. "I'm so glad to see you!"

"I'm glad to see you, too." Jenny pulled from her arms, slowly going to look at her babies sleeping in their bassinets in the den. "I knew you'd take good care of my children. They look wonderful."

But she didn't reach to touch the squirming bundles that were now starting to wail to be picked up and comforted.

"They don't like me," Jenny said, whirling to face Caleb and April.

"They don't know you. They just want to be held." April rushed to scoop up Matthew, whom she knew could be calmed the quickest, and thereby hopefully alleviate Jenny's worries. "See? Just as easy as can be."

"Not for me." Jenny shook her head. "I'd be afraid to pick them up. They're bigger than they were in the hospital, but they still look so fragile."

Caleb put two babies in his arms, sitting on the sofa with them. "They don't break, Jenny. But don't think about that right now. Let us just take care of you first. The babies are fine."

Refusing to sit down, Jenny finally met April's gaze. "I have to tell you something, April."

"Tell me. It's okay, whatever it is."

"The day I left, you'd put your sweater on your chair. You had some money in the pocket, I saw you put it there after someone paid you for picking up something. I took twenty dollars."

"Oh, Jenny," April said, relieved. "Thank you for telling me, but I didn't think a thing about it. I'm glad you had money. I was so worried you left without a dime. Please don't go anywhere without telling us. We were so worried about you!"

"Caleb said you were. That's why I agreed to

come back. I wanted you to know that I'm fine. In fact, I'm better than I thought I'd be.''

"And you'll be much better in the future. How about a piece of chocolate cake and a glass of milk?''

"I'm not hungry, thanks.''

Jenny went to stand by the window, looking out at the street. April had a chance to run a quick glance over the girl. She was dressed in jeans and a loose shirt. Her hair hung lankly, but it was clean. Other than seeming thin—and somewhat depressed—Jenny looked much better than she'd expected.

"February is such a gray month,'' Jenny murmured. "I'd forgotten how ugly Texas is in the winter. It's all concrete in the city.''

Caleb and April glanced at each other. He shook his head. Clearly, Jenny's reaction puzzled him as much as it did April. But she was a nurse—and a female. She should have some insight into Jenny, and unfortunately the girl just seemed so sad that it concerned April terribly. "Jenny, why don't you come sit down next to me.''

To her surprise, Jenny did, suddenly leaning her head on April's shoulder. "I miss David so much,'' she said. "I miss my husband, and I can't bear the thought that I'll never see him again. I'd give anything just to hear his voice one more time. And I can't stop thinking that if he hadn't taken that job to support me and the children, he wouldn't have gotten hurt. We'd have gone off to college, and he'd still be alive.''

Caleb's and April's eyes met in a sudden flash of realization. The problem went much deeper than postpartum depression, April realized. So much farther than deep grief.

''You can't understand what it's like to lose your best friend, the only one you ever had,'' Jenny said, talking out loud now to no one in particular.

FROM APRIL'S ROOM so he wouldn't wake Jenny who'd fallen asleep on the sofa, Caleb alerted the authorities, Social Services and the hospital that Jenny had been found, and that her health appeared reasonably good. He called Jackson to let him know as well.

''Fine work, son. I knew you'd find her.''

His father's praise was of no particular comfort to him. Whether Jackson meant to or not, Caleb always felt his dad was bringing up his past, trying to show him that he was a damn fine cop. Had been, and could be again.

Caleb wouldn't, and that was the way he wanted it. The second that Jenny had said that they couldn't possibly understand what it felt like to lose a best friend, the only one in the world, he'd known exactly how deep her suffering went.

''Does this mean your marriage is over? Since a mom and children reunion was the goal of the mission?'' his father asked him.

He rubbed his eyes, tired from the flights, and the emotional seesaw of picking Jenny up and bringing her home. The sadness in April's eyes was there, too, pulling on him, though she'd never admit she was going to be devastated to give up the babies. "I don't think it's going to be that easy, Dad."

"No? Is there a problem?"

"I think we underestimated Jenny's degree of depression. I'm no doctor, but I don't see a quick resolution on this matter."

He wondered if the sound he heard on the other end of the phone was Jackson rubbing his hands with glee. Closing his eyes wearily, he said, "You like April, don't you, Dad."

It was a statement of fact, not a question.

"I do, Caleb. She reminds me an awful lot of your mother. Gentle souls draw me, I suppose."

The last thing Caleb wanted was a woman as delicate and frail as his mother. "I'll talk to you later, Dad."

"Call me if I can help out in any way."

"I will. Bye."

Clicking his phone shut, he sat on April's bed, thinking for a moment. He was in this for the short term, and he had a bad feeling it had just turned into the long haul.

April walked into the room, softly closing the door behind her. "Jenny fell asleep on the sofa. I think it's best if she rests all she can."

"Definitely." He saw so many questions in

April's eyes that he didn't know where to start. "She was staying in the home of an elderly lady who had taken her in. She was fine, and she wasn't that hard to convince to come home. It was almost as if she was grateful to be brought back. I think she couldn't make herself do it on her own, and yet she knew she had to."

"We may have underestimated her situation," April said. "I feel foolish saying that, because as a nurse, I always think I can assess a patient's health fairly well, but this time I didn't."

"You're used to working with babies. They don't have issues. They poop, they sleep, they eat, they want to be held. Fairly simple in comparison to what Jenny's going through. There's no way you could have assessed that."

She sat on the bed next to him, staring into his eyes. "It occurs to me that you might be kicking yourself right now."

"For what?" he demanded.

"You made an offer to secure the babies for me. We'd bring the mother home, give her some time to adjust, make certain the children weren't separated or shuffled into undesirable situations, and then we'd…wrap up the case."

He nodded. "That's what we thought. Or at least, as close as it can be described."

She reached to touch his hand. "Has this turned into more than you bargained for?"

How could he tell her that he was falling for her—

had fallen for her—and yet, he had no right to? "This situation has forced me to evaluate my life. And myself. Who I am, and who I want to be."

Silently, she nodded. "What do you think happens now?"

"Are you asking me what I want to happen, or what I think will happen?"

"Does it matter? Can't it be one and the same?"

He shook his head slowly. "I don't think so."

Chapter Seventeen

With those words ringing in her ears, April knew her marriage was over. Caleb had never wanted something long term, and now that Jenny had returned, it was clear that nothing about her situation could be short term. He regretted the marriage bargain they'd made.

There was nothing she could say about that. The sound of her heart shattering was louder than any words she could speak anyway.

"Let's give her a night to sleep on everything," he suggested. "We're all tired. In the morning, we can figure out how we're all going to fit together."

She raised her gaze to his.

"There's not enough sleeping space here, for one thing," he reminded her. "We'll have to buy a cot or something. And since Jenny seems unable to care for her children, that presents a whole new problem."

"I'll make an appointment for her with a doctor

at Maitland. No doubt they will refer her to a clinical psychologist after assessing her general health.''

He nodded. "Social Services is going to want to talk to her as well. That's something we need to think about.''

"What do you think will happen when they realize she is unable, at the moment, to care for her babies?'' April couldn't help being concerned. She and Caleb were only approved as a temporary foster care arrangement.

"I hope that by the time Jenny talks to them, she's made some kind of recovery in her emotions. But if not, maybe we persuade Social Services that the best thing for the children is to be here, with us, where their mother can spend some time adjusting to them.''

April looked down at her hands. "Caleb, thank you for thinking all this through. And for helping her.''

He sighed. "I want to, April.''

"You do?''

"Yeah.'' He gave her the most serious look she'd ever seen him wear. "It's my chance to make up for a lot of things. And that's the way I see it. You have nothing to thank me for.''

They stared at each for a few moments, their eyes searching each other's. Then he said, "I'm going to run by my dad's and pick up a cot I just remembered he's got over there.''

"Okay." Silently, she wondered if the cot was for him or for Jenny, but she was too afraid to ask.

"YOU DIDN'T HAVE a boyfriend before I left," Jenny said when April came out of her bedroom. She'd waited to leave her room until she heard the closing of the front door. She hadn't wanted to watch Caleb leave. One day she'd have to watch him go out the front door, and know he'd never come in it again. "Much less a fiancé. As I recall, you didn't even mention a significant other."

"No, I suppose I didn't," April said.

"That was sure fast."

April looked at Jenny, who was perching on the sofa at an odd angle, as if she was trying to avoid looking at the bassinets that contained sleeping babies. Jenny had a soap opera running on television, a soft hum of voices punctuated every once in a while by a dramatic shriek. A tissue box lay propped against a pillow. "Some things happen quickly sometimes."

"You said once that you wanted children of your own someday, but that you hadn't met the right man. You met him in the space of a couple of months."

"Guess I was lucky. He's actually the brother of my best friend, so it wasn't all that far-fetched."

"Still."

April held her breath, hoping Jenny wouldn't ask any more questions.

"Did you marry him because I asked you to take care of my babies?"

How much truth and details could Jenny handle? Was any of it important?

"I'm not certain what the relevance of your question pertains to," April said honestly. "If you're asking me if I married Caleb because I needed help with your children, then the answer is no."

"Are you in love with him?"

"Why do you ask that?"

"Because people fall in love and get married. I don't know why, but I don't feel like that's what happened. Maybe you got married and are hoping to fall in love."

April tried to give a nonchalant shrug. "Maybe."

"Then if that's what happened, you did it after I left, because you didn't mention it beforehand. That means you did it because of me, because of the children."

"It's more complicated than that," April said, uncomfortable.

"I know you're trying to spare me, April. I know I haven't handled some things as well as I could, but this is something I can handle. I need to know because it affects everything."

"Everything?"

"Yes. If you're married to someone you don't love because of me, that's not fair."

April shook her head. "I can't answer your question."

"Can't, or won't?"

"Sincerely cannot."

Jenny drew in a deep breath. "Caleb says Social Services is going to ask me a lot of questions. He says that they're going to want me to be with my...with them. My babies."

"I think that's what we all want, Jenny. After you've had time to grieve, and some time to come to grips with everything, it might be what you want, too."

Caleb came back inside the house, startling both of them. He was windblown, and his ears were red, as were his cheeks.

"I thought you'd gone to get a cot," April said.

"I was leaving, when your neighbor's dog escaped," he said before going into the kitchen to warm up his hands with tepid water. "Little-bitty poodle thing, running for all it was worth across the street, and enjoying its freedom to the max. Unfortunately, the little boy who went running after it was extremely unhappy, and he knew better than to go into the street to get it." Caleb shrugged. "So I chased the damn dog to the next block before I finally tackled it."

"You tackled his puppy?" Jenny asked.

"I had to catch him. If he'd gotten run over, and I had to go tell that kid what had happened, I don't think I could have taken it. Damn it, but it's cold outside!"

He wasn't wearing a coat. April said, "What happened to your coat?"

"That's what I tackled the dog with. I threw my coat over it like a net, then sort of leaped to make certain the pooch didn't wiggle out and take off. Unfortunately, when I picked it up using the coat as a blanket—and a shield, I'm not too embarrassed to say—the damn dog peed on it."

April shook her head, trying very hard not to laugh. "I have never heard you say damn so many times in one conversation."

"I wish I'd seen it," Jenny said, the first smile she'd shown touching her lips. "I'll bet you were mad when it peed on your coat."

"It was a reflex action to wrap the dog in the coat after all the bundling I've been doing lately with these babies," he said sternly. "And I was no more mad at that dog than I am when the babies wet as soon as I get them diapered. Sometimes, the boys do it *before* I get the diaper on. I just vow to be a little quicker next time with them, but I told the little boy he'd have to find someone who was in better shape to chase his dog next time." He sank into a chair. "Forget the cot. I'll get it later. After I've recovered."

April laughed, but Jenny's face turned serious again. "Actually, Caleb," she said, "you don't have to get the cot. I called Mrs. Fox, and she said I was welcome to stay with her until I get back on my feet. For as long as I need to."

CALEB TOOK JENNY to Mrs. Fox's, promising to pick her up again the next day. He found himself driving to April's as fast as the speed limit would allow, knowing that they had to talk, and they had to talk a lot. There were some decisions that had to be made, and he wasn't certain either of them had the answers.

The aroma of something cooking greeted him at the door. April popped her head around the kitchen frame. "Your coat's clean now. It wasn't all that bad."

She'd washed his coat and cooked a meal. He liked it; he liked it very much. "Why aren't they yelling or squirming or crying?" he asked.

April came out of the kitchen. "All I can think of is that they're comforted by the sound of the TV. Jenny had it on this afternoon, and I left it on after she left. I guess it soothes them somewhat to hear quiet noise."

"Quiet noise. Now that's something to ponder." His stomach growled, and he decided to be very male about it. "Is that dinner I smell cooking? And am I invited?"

"It's dinner, and it's for the man who chases neighborhood puppies." April went back into the kitchen and Caleb followed, intrigued by her attempt to please him.

"I have no offering of my own. No bottle of wine, no box of candy."

"Baked chicken and rice isn't romantic, Caleb. It's just an easy dinner."

"I could run up to the store and get a bottle of wine."

"Sit down and watch TV. I'm going to tear some lettuce for a salad."

"I can do that." He further encroached upon her kitchen. "Mmm. And a cake."

"That was for Jenny. Yet, it didn't seem that a homecoming cake was warranted, considering how she feels about everything."

"Time is supposed to be the great healer." He stuck a fork into the chocolate cake, sighing with happiness. "My favorite. I could sit here and eat just this."

"Dinner's not for an hour. You want to?" April got herself a fork out of the drawer and sat across the dinette.

"Maybe it'll make the conversation we need to have a little sweeter."

"I don't think so. No matter what, we have to admit that our plan didn't work out the way we hoped."

"No. It didn't." He stabbed a forkful of cake and enjoyed it, his eyelids closing for a moment. "Have any suggestions?"

"Don't fill up on cake? Don't use your coat as a net?"

"That's about all I can come up with, too."

He put his fork down and looked at her. "Remember when I told you that running through the trails of the teenage mind was challenging?''

April raised an eyebrow. "Yes."

"Jenny told me in the car that there's no way she'll ever be able to see these newborns without feeling pain. She loves them, and she wants them to have what she cannot give them, but to her they represent a painful loss she wants to forget. She said those aren't the feelings a mother should have for her children.''

"She told you that?"

He nodded. "She left because she was frightened, she was out of her mind, but she was also too desperate to face the future alone, and she feels that she'll never be a good mother. She and David were too young to get pregnant, but with him, she could have done it. All those babies do is remind her of him. And it's not something she can face. Ever.''

"Oh my God. Poor Jenny. Poor babies."

"Exactly. She wants to sign them over to you and me for adoption. On two conditions. One, that we want them, and two, that we plan on staying married.''

April felt her heart drop straight into her stomach. She wondered what Caleb thought when he'd heard *that* pronouncement. "What did you tell her?"

"I told her I thought she needed to take some time to make such a drastic decision. She said it was only drastic to me, that she's been thinking about it ever since she left. She didn't want to come home with me, but she knew she had to face what she'd left behind, and do whatever legal work needed to be done for her children. When she found out you and I were married—that you actually had a spouse—it seemed like a gift from God.'' He spread his hands on the table. ''That's what she called our marriage, our family. A gift from God. An answer to her prayers.''

''Well.'' April sighed. ''We are certainly perpetuating a successful fraud then.''

''Her conditions beg an interesting question we certainly hadn't foreseen.'' He reached across the table, gently taking her fingers between his. ''First, April, you have to decide if raising these children is what you really want to do, for a long time. We had planned on a somewhat less extended situation.''

''True,'' she murmured, her heart hammering.

''We talked a lot about our own personal baggage a long time ago. Can you make a commitment to her children?''

''I can,'' April whispered, wondering if he meant a commitment without him.

''Then if you know that's what you can do and want to do, we have to move on to the second condition. Part of Jenny's motivation is that she wants the children to have what she never did, and what she cannot give them now—a stable, loving home with two married parents.''

April stared at him. He rubbed her fingers between his before touching the lovely engagement ring he'd given her.

"Do we want to be married to each other, all or nothing? Do or die? The real deal, the whole enchilada, close-the-escape-hatch type of married?"

The half smile on his face belied the seriousness of what was in his question. "I can't answer for both of us. But…" The secret she was keeping floated inside her consciousness, pressing her guilt buttons. "I don't know, Caleb. I know I'm not unhappy with what we have."

It seemed his features shifted in an expression she didn't have time to analyze, almost as if he was disguising his own feelings. "I'm not unhappy, either."

"But it's a lot for two people who don't know each other very well to decide on overnight."

"Exactly."

She thought he looked relieved. April wasn't sure what she was. "You know what, I think I'll go lie down for a while. If you don't mind eating alone, that is."

He wouldn't let her pull her fingers from his. "April."

"Yes?"

"Are you upset with me, or upset about the situation?"

"Both, I think," she said quietly. "But mostly with myself."

"Commitment-phobia?"

"I think so. I've never liked depending upon anyone, and I find myself needing you more and more."

"Because of the babies."

"Yes." Her head drooped. "I do like you, though, Caleb. Like Jenny, maybe all we need is time."

"What if time isn't the healer in this instance?"

She shook her head. "I don't know. I've just about run out of answers, while the questions just keep piling up."

Does he want to stay with me? Does he feel the same way about me I feel about him? Should I tell him how I feel? Should I tell him there's a chance we might be expecting more than quadruplets on our doorstep?

The questions piled up; the answers ran faster than puppies and a young mother and little baby fists and feet flailing the air.

In the morning, April awoke to two realizations: One, her brief lie-down had turned into seven hours of fitful sleep.

Two, she'd slept alone.

Chapter Eighteen

"You're here," she said with some surprise—and a lot of gladness—as she walked into the den. An adorably whiskered and jeans-and-T-shirt-clad Caleb sat with two babies in his arms, rocking them in one of the rockers he'd dragged from the nursery.

"These little darlings decided they'd party all night. They invited me, and I figured you needed the sleep."

She went to sit beside him on the sofa. "My turn. You go get some rest now."

"Now that Jenny's been located, I have no place pressing to be. No reason to snooze. It's probably best if you and I take a day to see how we feel about making a real marriage out of this."

"No ideas came to me in the night. You?"

"Nah. I think we have to give ourselves an A for effort now, and not worry about flunking the course."

April smiled. "Your approach to school was relaxed."

"Confident."

"Ah. You're confident about a lot of things."

"It's either face a crisis situation with confidence, or fold because you don't believe in yourself. If we stay married and look into adopting these children, April, I'm going to approach our marriage and our family with confidence."

He was so darn appealing when he looked stubborn about something. She wished Caleb wasn't quite as appealing as he was—it made it hard to think about a time when he might not be her husband.

On the other hand, if anyone was worth unpacking her baggage for, it was him. "How can you be so certain we're not taking advantage of Jenny's distress?"

"Because she's thought her dilemma through. She knows what she's capable of right now. I'd worry if we'd have the children in another town, but we won't. We'll be right close by whenever she wants to see the babies. In a way, I think this would be better because she could adjust to them without being so frightened and so overwhelmed."

"Remember what you said about me projecting my needs onto her?"

"Forget about it. I told you, I work through every angle of a case. What I know now about this case is that I think I understand Jenny very well."

"You do?"

"Now that I've talked to her a couple of times,

yes. It's not wrong for Jenny not to want to be a mother if she knows she can't do it without David, if she'd dread it horribly. We can't judge or predict her grief cycle. Only she knows best.''

''How do you know this so confidently?''

''Because it took me nearly all my life to give up a chunk of what was bothering me.'' He held up a hand to make a point. ''And still, it remains a part of me I can't forget. I don't know when I will, either.''

She thought about her elderly adoptive parents, and how much they had done for her. Without them, she might have never had a chance. ''I guess we do get over some things in time.'' Glancing at him shyly, she said, ''Caleb, I never saw myself as the type of woman to be a good wife.''

He shrugged, not waking the babies he held. ''I sure never saw myself as dad material. Believe me, me and the old man have gone a round or two that would lead you to believe that I'm lacking some parental training. If we learn by example, anyway.''

Her secret burned inside her. He was trying so hard to acclimate himself to the situation he'd had no part in making; only that he tried to make her happy. She couldn't bear to upset him, especially if it was for no reason.

''Let's take a few more days to think about it,'' she said.

''Worried that Jenny will change her mind?''

Worried that you will.

But she only smiled and began making breakfast. "I know what's wrong," she said suddenly, coming back into the room. "I know what I'm afraid of."

He looked at her.

"We're making it work, not celebrating it," she said. "Caleb, there's nothing wrong with realizing that this isn't what we started out thinking we were doing, and it's not what we'll celebrate. It should be the biggest moment of our lives."

"April," he said kindly, "you need a day off. Away from the babies. A day of pampering should be on your to-do list."

She gave him an impatient glare. "You're not listening to me."

"I am. I'll watch the babies if you want to go get your nails done. Maybe a massage, but not by one of those guys who makes a woman want him to remove her towel."

"You've lost *your* mind," she told him.

"I can't help it. I'd be a little jealous to think of another man near your nude body."

That stopped her. She'd been talking about his assertion that she needed a break. Jealous? Caleb? "Would you really?" she asked, fascinated by this emerging side of his personality.

"How did we get from you having cabin fever to me having a slight distrust of men who run their hands over women for a living?"

"You're sidestepping an issue you raised," she

pointed out, "as well as not being very politically correct, I might add."

"Since when is it politically incorrect to be slightly jealous? Very, very minutely, I might emphasize."

"Never mind," she said with a sigh. "Can we get back to celebrating? My point is that we've sewn this little piecemeal family together with our love and our heartstrings. We've done something pretty good, Caleb."

"Do you want me to take you out to dinner? We could pop a bottle of bubbly?"

She smiled at his tentative offer. "It's more an emotional celebration I mean. But thank you. I'll definitely take you up on some bubbly another time. I had a phone call from Bri yesterday, by the way."

"And what did my sister have to say?"

"She filled me in on the latest gossip. It's probably what's got me thinking maybe we've pressed so much into our situation that we haven't taken the time to examine if we're happy about it."

"Bri is a troublemaker," he grumbled, his tone loving in spite of the words.

"She told me that Adam and Maggie are finally going to have the baby they've longed for. It's a wonderful blessing, because you know that Adam and Maggie have undergone so many trials with the fertility treatments that their marriage had begun to show some stress. But now they'll be a family. Sometimes people don't know how they're going to get to be the family they want so much, but it should be celebrated when it happens. You're going to be an uncle again, Caleb."

"Well, isn't that something," he said, enormously pleased. "Another baby in the family."

She smiled, her lips stretched to simulate pleasure for the news, but all she could do was hope that he'd be as pleased when she told him *her* news.

Their news. She had a feeling he wouldn't want to celebrate, then.

THEY SPENT a fast morning with the babies keeping them on the go. Caleb was starting to think he could handle this project pretty well: four babies and a wife. Maybe he could do this permanent-marriage thing as good as he'd ever done anything he'd tried.

The instant he thought about the marriage as a project, he knew April had a point. One of them was assuming a life he'd never seen for himself out of a sense of duty.

"You're right," he said suddenly. "Maybe I've been on autopilot."

She paused in the act of bending over a bassinet to check on Craig. Her head turned to stare at him, and he couldn't help thinking that it would kill him not to see that spunky face every day. That tousled auburn hair alone felt like silk to his hungry fingertips.

"Autopilot for you is to serve, protect and defend," she said. "I think that's just what you've been doing, for us. And as long as that's the case, I don't think I have anything to offer you that you'll let me give you, Caleb.''

He hadn't expected her to read his feelings. Chewing on the inside of his jaw, he said, ''I suppose the healer in you has a suggestion?''

''Maybe.''

When she bent over like that, making her hair hang forward a little, and then shot him that teasing smile that said oh so clearly that his smart-aleck question hadn't rattled her, he had a suggestion of his own. He desperately wanted to put that woman back in her white bed and christen it for their own. ''I'm listening. Let me hear your best shot.''

''I think you miss the police force like crazy. And I think you've put us in the place of what you're missing.''

He stared at her.

She gave him an innocent look as she stood up. ''You're not the only one who runs through every angle, Caleb. I was a pretty good nurse, and I'm a very astute woman.''

The wink she gave him was unsettling. He wasn't certain if he liked realizing he'd met his match. She'd hit the bull's-eye, dead center. ''I guess you'll have a diagnosis, Nurse Sullivan?''

Her shrug was way too unassuming. ''Talk to someone at the force about how you feel. I've never heard you mention that you talk with anyone, Caleb.

And I know you don't talk to me. You're too busy trying to take care of me, the babies, Jenny.''

''Are we back to that independence thing?''

''No.'' She gave him a smile that was somehow sad, somehow knowing. ''But I do think you need to give some thought to how much your partner's death impacts how close you'll want to be to this family. And to me.''

He sighed, the tone unwilling even to his ears.

''You can't receive love if you're not willing to, Caleb.''

''Do you want to give it to me?''

''Maybe,'' she retorted. ''But I'm not going to force it on a man who slips into my bed at night and then skitters away before dawn.''

''I was trying to be considerate.''

''And I liked having you in my bed. I just think you've got to want to stay in it, all the way.''

''Are you suggesting you wouldn't mind if I went back to my old life?''

''I want whatever you want. But I want you to do what you want, instead of living with fear and regret. You won't be any better off than Jenny if you do.''

''Technically frozen.''

''Right. Her grief is fresh, though. You and I owe it to these kids to move on.''

''I'll think about it,'' he said, wanting it to be way down on his to-do list.

She gave him that foxy smile as she bent over

Matthew's bassinet, and he decided maybe he'd think about it sooner than later.

"SO, YOU'RE NOT THINKING about returning to cop work," Andrew Mulligan, Caleb's former captain and close friend, said offhandedly.

"I don't think so. But it is a big part of me that will always be there."

"Sure. We can use you if you think the time is right."

Caleb wasn't certain of anything. His old life, his new wife and the in-between-the-two knife that had once seemed to separate the two so clearly. "I've got these four children now," he said with some wonder.

"I heard. I also heard that you're the one who brought the missing mom back."

"Yeah." He nodded, feeling satisfaction with his part in bringing Jenny successfully to her children. Initially, he'd been afraid that she'd resist returning, but somehow a bond had forged between them. She trusted him. It was a matter of time before she began to trust her love for her children. She'd never be equipped to handle the emotional needs of the quads—were there any single teenage parents who could?—but one day she'd find her footing with them. And sometimes that was enough.

"You're a great cop, Caleb."

Present tense. The past was still a part of him. "My dad always says it just that way, Andrew."

"The old man's right. You are. I just sense your heart's not in it anymore."

"No. I don't think it really is." Yet there was still something there, a question unsolved.

"Your new family will begin to replace your relationship with Terry," Andrew said softly. "In case you're wondering if there's light at the end of the tunnel after losing a partner."

"How do you know?"

Andrew shrugged. "I know."

"Okay." Caleb accepted that, hearing the deeper edge in Andrew's voice and knowing that personal experience was speaking.

"By the way, Terry's wife is dating again. Did you know that?"

His skin prickled with electricity. "Dana is dating?"

"Yeah. A real good cop, too. Something wrong with that?" Andrew asked with a patient smile.

"No. I guess not. I mean, I guess I just…"

"It's been a few years," Andrew said gently. "She'll always grieve for Terry, but she has a family to think about. She knew it was best to move on."

Caleb didn't know what to think about that. Had it been that long since that fateful night? So long, and yet it seemed like yesterday.

"Let go of the guilt, Caleb," Andrew said softly. "We've replayed that night a hundred times. All the officers in the area said the same thing. You did exactly what a good cop should have been doing. No one could have saved him.''

"I keep seeing it, thinking I could have moved faster, should have covered better," Caleb said, his voice uncertain.

"Anytime an officer is lost, we go over the details, debriefings, and every other angle to learn what went wrong, and what can be done better in the future. From what I read and heard, you saved a few other lives that night. Just not his. And sometimes, no matter how much we want it to be different, it's just out of our hands.''

"Maybe.''

"Some things *are* in our hands, though,'' Andrew said. "This marriage of yours, for one thing. Terry would want you to be happy, Caleb. And it sounds like you've got a helluva good thing going.''

"April's pretty sweet,'' Caleb admitted. "And those babies are something else.''

"Like 'em, do you?''

"They've turned me inside out pretty good.''

"Think of them as making up for your partner, if you need to, then,'' the captain told him. "Think of everything they're going to need emotionally that you're in a prime position to provide. Consider it a gift to Terry. He'd want that, you know.''

Terry had felt damn strongly about kids, that was for certain. He'd felt damn strongly about drugs on the streets that got into kids' hands, which was one of the reasons he'd been such a fierce warrior.

"You're right," Caleb said, feeling the past recede from focus. It was as if the present became crystal clear to him in that moment, and everything he wanted and needed and hoped to have in the future.

April. And the quads. And helping Jenny walk through the burning wall of grief until she could make it to the other side. Not as a parent, maybe, but as a whole person.

"Thanks, Andrew."

"You're welcome. Anytime. By the way, this conversation hasn't been totally unselfish on my part."

Caleb settled a gaze on him. "April doesn't have any unmarried sisters, Captain."

Andrew laughed, not offended in the least. "No. I'm not cut out for the job you're undertaking, Caleb. I was thinking of something more force-specific."

"As in?"

"I know you're working for your dad, but we could use a crack detective on the odd case," the captain said. "There's simply no one that works the angles and brings in the goods the way you do. It would be occasional, and I'd make certain only the real knuckle-crackers came your way. You'd be off the street and safe from harm, because I think we both agree that with four children, you'd better keep your head down. But you'd still have the opportunity to do something that's close to your heart, and that you're damn good at.''

A chance to do what he really loved again. Police work. It would mean spending less time working for his father, but no one would be happier than Jackson if he returned to what he was best at. Relief spread through him that he'd never expected to feel again, and a well of need opened up inside him.

For April.

She'd understood exactly what he needed to do. Suddenly, he felt healed.

Chapter Nineteen

Caleb hurried home to see April, to tell her that he understood it all now. She'd been right. Until he'd put the past away, he'd been simply giving, and not allowing her to give to him. It was as if he'd shoveled in all the dismay and guilt he'd carried into her life, like a giant piece of earthmoving equipment.

He was ready to be a partner rather than a martyr.

To his surprise, April was gone. So were the quads.

Maybe she'd gone to see Jenny. Quickly, he rang Mrs. Fox's house, asking to speak to Jenny.

"Hey, Caleb."

"Hey. Is April over there?" Maybe she'd taken the babies to Jenny, to try to get them together in small, easy-to-manage doses.

"No. I haven't heard from her, either."

"Oh."

"Caleb, I've been thinking about something."

"Go."

"I do want to be a part of my babies' lives."

His eyebrows raised. "That's great."

"But I still want you and April to adopt them. It's just that...I'm still at the age where I wish I could be adopted," she said quietly. "I wish I had a family who wanted *me*. Y'know? It's not that I can never love them, it's just that...I think you guys are what I would have wanted if I'd been able to have parents of my own."

"I'm so glad you explained your feelings to me," he said. "It helps a lot, Jenny. I don't think I'd ever quite seen it that way before, but don't worry about that anymore. April and I will be there for you. Consider yourself part of our family."

"Thanks, Caleb," she said softly, her voice teary with gratitude. "You've taken on an awful lot for me."

"I've gotten a lot, too. I'll come by and get you later so you can see the babies."

"I want to."

"Good. And then we'll talk about your future, and what we can do to help you."

"Thanks."

He hung up, strolling into the kitchen to look for a note from April. But there was nothing there, either. She could have gone to see Jackson, or Bri.

But packing up four newborns by herself required a mission, he was pretty certain. If there'd been an emergency with one of the children, she would have called his cell phone. Whatever it was, it didn't seem that she wanted him to know about it—just yet.

"Mom, Dad," she said to her adoptive parents as they stared at the newborns in their carriers. "I haven't told you the one-hundred-percent truth. This is Craig, Melissa, Chloe and Matthew, and it looks as though I will be officially applying for them to be my children."

It was clear that Donna and Webb were thunderstruck, as they sat on the high-backed green antique sofa, with a fan of babies in front of them. April felt terrible for not telling them the truth about her marriage sooner. As a short-term solution to Jenny's problem, she hadn't seen a need to bring it up. Now she realized that her decision had been pretty narrow-minded and selfish. They were her parents.

She'd been dutiful, but not loving. She'd shut them out of her life to the extent that she could. Adopting her as a teenager had been a leap of faith for them. Too afraid of a bond being ripped from her again, she'd protected her heart instead of allowing herself to be close to them.

She was a fine one to tell Caleb he needed to resolve his past unless she resolved hers as well.

"I wasn't totally honest with you. Caleb and I didn't get married as a love match." She swallowed, touching the cameo at her neck that her mother had given her on her wedding day. "We did it so we could apply for these children for temporary foster care."

"So these children are not Caleb's?" Donna asked.

"No. He married me so that we would have a two-parent home in order to secure temporary care, if possible. A girl who had come to the hospital bonded with me, and after she gave birth to these children, she sneaked out of the hospital. She left a note that asked me to take care of her children."

"And so you have, it appears," Webb said. "You have a kind heart, April, which other people see. But temporary and permanent are two different things, and Caleb isn't here with you, so it leads one to worry."

"Well, we weren't expecting the situation to need to become permanent. We thought that once Caleb found Jenny—he used to be a police officer and his father asked him to make use of some of his skills— Jenny would see her babies and fall in love with them."

"As you had," Donna commented.

"Yes," April admitted. "I couldn't imagine not falling for these children. They're all so special, they all have their unique moments. Craig impatiently waves his fist when he wants something. Matthew wrinkles his nose when he cries, Melissa can kick her feet like a Rockette and Chloe stretches her fingers as if one day she'll get whatever she wants on her own, without asking for help. Yes. I loved these children from the start."

"What about Caleb?" Webb asked.

"My feeling is that he's still in shock. He's offered to stay with me, but I'll know when the time is right to take him up on his offer."

"Do you love him?" Donna asked.

April bowed her head a little. "I do. I have for so long. But it's so easy to fall in love with a man like Caleb, Mom. He takes care of me and the babies so sweetly. And it's not just us. He went running off after my neighbor's puppy the other day. And he worries about Jenny. There's not a woman on earth who wouldn't appreciate what he has to offer."

"You don't want to be a burden," Webb stated.

"No," she said, shaking her head sadly. "I don't."

Her parents glanced at each other before Donna spoke. "That was always your number-one worry once we adopted you, April."

"It was?"

"Yes." She nodded. "Other girls your age thought about boys and dances and cheerleading. You thought about how you could help around the house, and worried about what scholarships you could get to colleges, so you wouldn't be a burden to us." Donna smiled at her a bit wistfully. "We wanted you to be a child, but it was as if you came into our home already an adult, feeling that you had to care for us."

"I did feel that way," April said uncertainly.

"We were patient with you, realizing that your situation had made you feel uneasy in our home,"

Webb said. "And we've always been proud of you. Very proud."

"Maybe you should be willing and comfortable with your answer if you ever feel that Caleb is asking you to stay with him because he wants you, honey, not because you're a responsibility he's shouldering. We certainly didn't feel that way," Donna told her gently.

"I feel like I'm starting all over today," April said, surprised. "I don't know why I didn't see any of this clearly, but I'm starting to feel like I didn't know you very well. That I didn't give you a chance. Is it possible to be born again? Because that's the way I feel."

Donna and Webb smiled at her.

"Hello, baby girl," Webb said. And then he held out his arms to her.

Without hesitating, April rose up on her knees and clasped her father's neck. Then she moved to kiss her mother on both cheeks. "I love you," she told her mother. "Thank you so much for being my mother, and knowing just what I needed to hear."

"It's what I always wanted to say," Donna said, "but I just knew it wasn't the right time. You needed to make your own way. And now, you have. Congratulations on your beautiful children, April. You'll make a fine mother. And a wife."

"It means so much to hear it," she whispered. "You can't know how much I've worried that I'd be unable to be a good wife."

Donna slowly got onto her knees beside April so that she could take a better look at the babies. "You'll be a wonderful mother now that you've let go of the past, too." She touched her daughter's hair with a trembling hand. "A word of caution, my sweet. The adoption process will be arduous."

"Was it?" she asked Webb, who rustily got down on his knees to peer into Matthew's carrier.

"It was," he confirmed. "But it was worth every minute. Look what we got, after all."

He took her hands in his, squeezing them for just a minute.

"Well, Webb," Donna said to her husband as he sat on the opposite side of April. "We always prayed for grandchildren."

The three of them looked at the carriers. Donna clasped her hands in delight. "I don't know how, and I don't know why, but the day I saw you standing in the orphanage, April, I knew you'd be the best daughter a mother could ever have. Four grandbabies! I can't wait to tell my church prayer group!"

CALEB FLEW OUT the door when he heard April's car pull into the driveway. He pulled open her door, unable to wait for her to get out of the car. "I was so worried!"

"Why?" April smiled at him, a new emotion for him residing in her heart. "We just went for an outing."

"That was some outing! It seemed you were gone for hours."

And there was a different air about her, a seeming peacefulness he'd never seen before. He liked it; she wore contentment well. "You didn't go see a masseur, did you?" he asked gruffly, unstrapping two of the baby carriers in the back seat.

"No." April laughed, the sound carefree and joyful to his ears.

"Well, whatever you did you look like it did you a whole lot of good. Stand there for a second with the other two while I take these little guys inside. I don't want you doing any more lifting than you've already done today."

He carried Matthew and Craig inside out of the chilly breeze. Returning to the car, he lifted out Melissa and Chloe, whom April had already unstrapped. Silently, they both went inside the little house, and each began unbundling babies and putting them on a puffy quilt on the floor.

Awkwardly, he wondered if she'd go ahead and mention where she'd been. It was about to kill him! For a man as good at figuring things out as he liked to boast that he was, he had no idea where she had taken the quads. After an hour had passed after his return—and he'd talked to the captain a while—he'd called his sister to ask surreptitiously nosy questions.

Bri had had the nerve to laugh at him. "Are you going to make a habit of calling me every time April gives you the slip? I'm going to install caller ID if you are."

He'd hung up, disgruntled, but only because Bri was the only one who would dare to call him on what he was doing—and then tease him about it. Deciding that he'd just have to wait, he had thrown himself onto the sofa, making certain his cell phone was on and nearby. Just in case.

"I went to see my old captain," he said, deciding the onus was on him to put April's concerns about him at rest. Where she'd been might forever be a mystery to him, but if she always returned looking that renewed, he'd let her go without question.

"You did?"

He sat up a little straighter, realizing he had her complete attention. "Yeah. I'm going to start doing an occasional case."

"What does that mean, exactly?" She wrinkled her nose at him, and he thought she looked just like Matthew when she did it.

"Detective work. Nothing big."

"It sounds big. It sounds like something you'd be very good at."

Her praise felt great. "The captain seems to think so."

"I think so, too. What did your dad say?"

"Congratulations. But he was very quiet, and when he's like that, I know he's trying to disguise his emotions. Dad had wanted me to go back to what he thought I was naturally good at for a long time. I'd resisted his encouragement.''

"Well, you and I have something in common, then." She folded a baby blanket and looked up at him. "I've been known to resist a little encouragement myself."

"Did the babies enjoy the outing?"

"They slept mostly. But when they were awake, they were darlings. Totally."

She smiled at the babies on the blanket beside her, and Caleb's heart warmed like a sea in warm summer. He pulled her up into his lap, but she surprised him, straddling him instead of reclining against him.

"I missed you," he said.

"I missed you more," she told him.

"I want you."

It had to be him who said it, April knew. She would have waited forever to hear those words from this man, because it was so important that he want her, because of everything that came with her. "I want you more."

"I have condoms," he told her, "if you're of a mind to tell the children we're going to take a nap."

"Condoms?" April looked down into his eyes from her perch in his lap.

"And champagne. I went by the store today because I agree with you, April. We should be celebrating."

"Oh, Caleb," she murmured, sinking into his outstretched arms. "I feel like it's the Fourth of July in February."

"Not New Year's all over again?" he asked, pulling her down on top of him on the sofa so that he could touch her hair, her face, her breasts.

"No," she said against his lips. "We've both moved forward, and that calls for a hotter, more intense holiday."

"Firecrackers work for me." With great speed, he pulled her sweater over her head and undid her jeans.

"I'm thinking Roman candles in February is perfect." Stripping off his jeans and pushing them down over his hips, she worked them off him until he was as nude as she was.

"You're beautiful," he said, taking hold of the blanket over the back of the sofa. "Too bad I have to cover you, but I don't want you cold, and I don't want to shock the children."

"The children appear too ready to sleep to care about watching us," April said, sighing as Caleb's mouth closed over her breast. She reached between his legs, massaging him, already wanting him.

"I've got to get the condoms," he said, splashing cold water on the shooting emotions inside her. "I don't want to take any chances on getting you pregnant."

It was so hard to stop the magic she was feeling, but she had to be honest with Caleb. He'd gone to the captain as she had suggested. He was making an honest attempt to put the past behind him.

Only she held the key to knowing if it ever truly would be. Sitting up, she wrapped the blanket around her as she stared down at him. "There's something I have to tell you."

She had to. No easy way to put it, either.

"Can it wait? It'll only take me a second to jog down the hall, babe. I promise it's going to be worth the wait."

She smiled and shook her head. "You've been so good to me, and to Jenny, and to the children." Her breath came deep from inside her as she pulled up courage. "It involves our marriage. The question of whether we want it to be a permanent marriage. There's only one thing I think we have to work out between us." She hesitated, but only for a second. "I know how you feel about having a child with me, Caleb."

The look on his face was not forthcoming. Instinctively, he had an idea where she was going with this.

"April, I would give you anything. I would do anything for you. It's not you. I don't want to have a child of my own with *anyone*."

Her secret forced her to probe the conversation more deeply. "Caleb, could you at least consider it?"

He shook his head.

"I think it's probably no secret to anyone that I've always wanted—"

His back went straight as he jumped up from the sofa and began putting on his clothes with unyielding haste. "What you want I cannot give you. I cannot give anyone. I will not *do* to anyone."

She frowned. "Caleb, please. You're not leaving any room for—"

But she'd pushed him too far, far past his breaking point. "No. The answer is no today, it will be no tomorrow, it will always be no. I thought you accepted me the way I was, the way I accepted you, April, past hurt and all. I can't really explain the depth of why I feel the way I do, but it's me, it's etched in my soul, dug in like damaged cells, and I'm never going to be any man but the one I said I was in the beginning. Like Jenny, there are some things a person only marginally heals from, and this is something I cannot do. I'm sorry. I'm really, really sorry." He took a deep breath, his face hard, his body nearly rigid from the assault of her plea. "And now, I'm leaving."

Chapter Twenty

"Please don't leave like this," April told Caleb as he tossed his things into a duffel bag.

It wasn't that he wanted to, but there was too much fear in him. He'd fallen in love with her—and it scared the hell out of him. She had needs he could not fulfill, needs she had a right to have fulfilled by someone. Not him. "I'm sorry."

She started to sob, wrenching his heart in two. "You care about me. I know you do."

True. That was, precisely, the problem. He'd meant to alleviate her needs, take care of her and the children. He'd never meant to start needing her the way he knew he did. And he'd meant to only give to her—but this, what he knew she really wanted, he could not give. He saw it in her face every time she held the adorable quads; he knew the depth of love in her soul. "I do. But I just can't get you pregnant, April. I could be responsible for you and the babies, because we thought it was short-term. And then it was a question of long-term, and that seemed possible, and maybe even right. But you're safe now," he said, his voice pleading for her to understand what even he could not explain. "I'll always be around to help you with all of this, just not in a husband capacity."

"I think I'm pregnant," she said hoarsely, her face torn with the agony of finally revealing her secret.

His whole being stilled in the act of jumping off the emotional cliff he'd been heading for. *"What?"*

"I think I'm pregnant. I'm not certain, but there's a possibility. I've got an appointment at Maitland tomorrow for accurate testing." This time the words were a hushed confession. She wiped her eyes, staring at him.

So helpless. And so sweet.

And so deeply embedded in him.

Coward if he jumped now; thief if he ran with her heart; bastard if he deserted her.

April would be such an awesome mother to his child. She'd already proved herself as a mother, so Madonna-like.

And yet so fragile.

"We need you," she said.

His mind blew into darkness, the impact tearing a crater in his soul.

Of course he'd been drawn to the gentle mother in her. She was, in so many ways, a frame for the delicate mother he'd never known.

There was too much pain swimming in his head.

So he sat down, tugged her into his lap, and, burying his face in her hair, burst into tears he'd never before allowed himself to cry.

"I know what I've been doing," he said finally as she silently wiped his tears away from his eyes with her fingertips. Her loving action was the final push to break down his wall of reserve. "I haven't been honest. I've been in love with you since the day I met you."

"Oh, Caleb," she said, her panic beginning to recede. His gaze was so clear, so honest, that she knew for the first time she was seeing the real him. All of him.

"I do love you," he told her.

"I love you, too," she whispered.

"I think I was taking the easy way out. We'd get married on a pretense. I knew in my heart Jenny couldn't handle the children, it was too much for her after losing her husband. She wanted you to have them, and then, so did I." He drew a deep, shuddering breath. "But I have to admit that I must have been trying to create a family without..."

April touched his face with her hand. "Endangering me?"

He stared into her eyes. "I'm so sorry. I admit my mom dying when I was born is a fact that has haunted me. Badly. It's not very brave, is it?"

"I think you're a hero," she said softly. "I love you more, as of this moment." Then she tapped her finger against his lips in a gentle rebuke. "But,

Caleb, if I am pregnant, can I just remind you of one thing?''

He nodded slowly.

"I am a nurse. I can take care of myself. *Good* care of myself. That's something you can't do for me."

She felt a ripple go through him. "I know. And I know it will be all right. But I'll still be scared."

Then he smiled at her, and she knew he had made peace with his past. "You can pace in the waiting room."

"I'll be right there in the delivery room with you. You should know that by now!"

It was true. He had been with her through some of the hardest, darkest moments. "I know. And I love you for it."

"And I love you, Nurse Sullivan-McCallum. But if you don't mind, I'm going to have to insist upon moving you and all these children into a bigger castle. With many bedrooms, and many bathrooms, and many phone outlets for the teen years. It won't be quite a dollhouse, but I give you my word that you can decorate it any way you please. Pink flowers, teacup wallpaper in the kitchen, I don't care. Five children! And I was the guy who said I wouldn't have any. Bri is going to tease me *unmercifully*." He groaned, but his face was happy. "Let's start looking for the perfect house, just the right thing for us—and our growing family."

"That's fine," she said with a smile, drawing his

head to hers for a kiss. "I was scared, too. I'm not anymore, Mr. Troubleshooter. And I'm ready to make that move with you."

"FALSE ALARM," April told Caleb as she snuggled up against him later that evening.

With the reading lamp on, Caleb was lying in her bed, bare-chested above a white sheet, as if he'd always done this before. He'd been circling real-estate ads in the newspaper, but he dropped the paper at her announcement, and sat up straight. "Really?"

"Really." And then she laughed.

"What's so funny?"

"I used a cop term, and you didn't even notice."

"Because it elicited the same kind of relief I'd always felt whenever I heard *false alarm*."

"But you seemed so surprised. If I didn't know better, I'd think you were disappointed, Caleb."

He thought about that a moment, realizing he'd been ready for whatever had come to them. That was the difference between then, and now.

He was ready.

Taking April in his arms, he said, "Nah. Hearing you talk cop to me turned me on, babe. I suggest we practice babymaking often and see where that takes us. *Stat.*"

She moaned underneath him, her need for him thrilling him. "Very funny, Caleb. A medical term. I got it."

"I'm so glad," he whispered, taking her with him, "I'm so glad that I've got you, to have and to hold. *Forever.*"